I0457601

Talisman of Light

Highland Hearts Afire
Time Travel Romance

By
B.J. Scott

Duncurra LLC

www.duncurra.com

Copyright 2017 by B.J. Scott

ISBN: 978-1-942623-43-4

Cover Art by Earthly Charms

Produced in the USA

Dedication

To my husband Steve.
Your unwavering love, encouragement, and support
make my writing dreams possible.

.

Acknowledgements

In addition to my husband and family, I want to thank my awesome Street Team for all their continued support and dedication to getting the word out about my books and for offering suggestions when called upon.

Thanks to Debby McCreary PA for your friendship and for keeping me grounded and focused when things get rough.

Thanks to Kathryn Lynn Davis for sharing your writing expertise.

And a huge thank you to Susan Cusack and all of the staff at Duncurra LLC for the hard work and dedication it takes to get a book published.

Finally, I want to thank my readers. Without you, there would be no need for books.

Scotland, a country steeped in legend, myths and superstition.

A place where anything can happen if you are willing to suspend disbelief and dare to dream.

The Legend
of the Talisman of Light

Eons ago, the winter hag, the immortal Cailleach, who held power over the seasons decided she wanted eternal youth. She worked for centuries to discover the magic that would make this possible. Finally, she learned an ancient spell, that if worked correctly, just after midnight on Imbolc would give her the youth and beauty she desired.

However, there was one troubling detail. The magic required the life of a young woman, but not just any young woman. For the spell to work she required an oldest daughter or a youngest daughter, a virgin pure of heart, who had lived no less than eighteen and no more than twenty-one summers. And she couldn't just steal the lass away, the lass herself had to come willingly.

The young woman would be sacrificed in the sacred well just after midnight on Imbolc and the Cailleach would be able to steal her youth. One full year for each year of the girl's life.

Knowing that no mortal would make such an offering unless a greater peril loomed, the old hag's power gave her just such a threat to level. She told the mortals that she would keep her icy grip on the land, preventing spring from coming and locking them in eternal winter unless they offered a sacrifice. She went a step further, marking the lass who best met the criteria and demanding that she willingly offer herself to save her people.

Even though the people knew the Cailleach would demand another girl when the spell wore off, they didn't see another way. Desperate to save his daughter, the father of one the chosen girls sought the aid of a Druid priestess. She bid him to bring her a special stone.

"Tonight, take your daughter to the river. Have her dig her fingers in the mud at the water's edge until she finds a stone and bring it straight to me. From the cold and the dark, I will create light."

The man did just as she asked, returning to her later that night with the stone his daughter had selected.

The Druidess laid the stone on the ground and built a sacred fire over it. When it was burning high and hot, she placed a single branch of rowan in the blaze. Glorious crimson flames leapt skyward. And as the Druidess chanted incantations through the night, the fire continued to burn as if by magic, for the woman added no more fuel to it.

Then, just as dawn pinked the sky, the fire died. It looked as if the ground had simply swallowed it. But where it had burned, lay a ruby, as brilliant as the flames from which it was born. The Druidess handed the man the gem, along with a silver chalice. "Make this into a talisman and drop it into the sacred well. Tell the Cailleach that she need only drink from the cup just after midnight on Imbolc and the talisman of light will give her a season of youth."

"A season of youth?"

"Aye, she will become young and beautiful instantly and remain so through midsummer. After that she will begin to age again, returning to her ancient form by Samhain."

"But why would she agree to that? If my daughter offers her life, the hag will have eighteen years of youth."

"True, but then she'll need another appropriate sacrifice. And someday, there may not be a willing young woman who meets all the criteria. Then she will not only lose her youth forever but her immortality as well. If she drinks the water every year at Imbolc, the talisman allows the rhythm of the seasons to renew her every year for eternity."

The man made the talisman as instructed and waited at the well, with his daughter on the eve of Imbolc. When the

Cailleach arrived, he showed her the gem and told her what the Druidess had said.

Just as he expected, the Cailleach laughed and asked, "Why would I accept a single season of youth once a year over eighteen years of it?"

"Because the Druidess foresees a time when there may not be a pure, willing lass of the age you seek. And when that time comes you'll lose your immortality."

This gave the Cailleach pause and she agreed.

However, over time the Cailleach grew greedy. She didn't want just a season of youth, she wanted perpetual youth, but the only way for that to happen was for her to steal it from a young woman as she had originally planned. And if the time came when a suitable sacrifice was not available, she would resort back to the water from the sacred well.

So, she removed the talisman and hid it. She announced to the people that the amulet had been stolen from the well and to prevent an eternal winter, it must be returned or a sacrifice made. Imbolc was but a few days away.

Again the people had a brief reprieve. A healer in the village came forward. She had just filled a cask with water from the well to use for healing potions before the talisman had disappeared. She offered to save it and give enough to the hag each year to work her spell for as long as the water lasted. The people hoped to find the lost talisman of light before the water ran out but they feared it wouldn't be possible. So they selected a young woman who would meet the requirements. A Dunmore lass.

Chapter One

Alex Innes stared out the window, but the dark clouds enveloping the plane were so dense, he couldn't see the wing. They'd been circling Inverness International Airport, waiting for the snowstorm to lift for what seemed like an eternity. He had always dreamed of visiting the fishing village of Burghead, the Innes Clan's ancestral home on the northern shore of Scotland, but right now, the only thing he wanted was to have his feet planted firmly on the ground.

"This has been a brutal winter." An elderly woman sitting in the seat next to Alex touched his forearm. "I was just telling my husband that I canna remember a worse one."

"Dinna be bothering the man," her husband grumbled.

"No bother." Thankful for the distraction, Alex offered them both a smile. "The sun was shining when I left J.F.K International in New York City, and the temperature was an unseasonably mild forty-three degrees. But I'm accustomed to harsh winters. Growing up in rural Connecticut, I've seen my share of Nor'easters blow up the New England coast."

On many occasions, he'd trudged through a few feet of snow on his way to school, had shoveled driveways to earn extra cash, and loved cross-country skiing. But his fondest memories were of ice-fishing in the local creek with his dad. He closed his eyes and could hear the crunch of snow beneath his feet, could feel the sting of crisp winter air on his cheeks, and could almost taste the gingerbread cookies and peppermint-laced hot chocolate his mother always sent along for them to enjoy. Reminiscing about his childhood provided a great source of comfort, but the brief moment of solace was interrupted by gut-wrenching fear when the plane began to rock and pitched.

Alex swallowed hard against the lump of bile rising in

his throat. At thirty-one, he still had many things he wanted to do. Honoring a deathbed request from his father and returning an ancient amulet to its intended resting place in Scotland topped his list.

He withdrew the small velvet pouch he'd hidden in the breast pocket of his leather jacket and clenched his fist around it. If the enclosed relic possessed the protective power his father claimed, he could surely use it now. He was not a superstitious man, but as an archeologist, he'd studied cultures and the ancient beliefs of people from all over the world, including the legends of his own ancestors.

"Can I have your attention please?" A flight attendant appeared at the front of the cabin and shifted her weight from one foot to the other. "Please fasten your seatbelts and make sure your tables are in the upright position." Despite her effort to remain calm and professional, she failed to hide the nervous tremor in her voice. "We are experiencing a bit of turbulence, but the tower has assured the pilot that the worst of storm has passed, and the runway has been cleared for our landing. Please remain in your seats until we have touched down. Thank you for flying Highland Airways. I hope you enjoy your visit to Scotland and will fly with us again soon."

"Na bloody likely. Next time we visit my sister in Glasgow, we're taking the train," the elderly gentleman said to his wife, snaking his arm around her shoulder. "I've a good mind to write the airline a letter of complaint."

The woman patted her husband's forearm. "It's na the airline who controls the weather, Angus. You must trust in the Lord to see us safe." She glanced at Alex. "Is that na true, young man?"

"I'm sure everything will be just fine." Alex hoped to reassure the couple, but had to admit, the same thoughts had crossed his own mind. He'd never been fond of flying, but as the head of the Archeology Department at a prestigious New York University, he travelled often with his students to foreign countries. Going by air was the swiftest, most practical way to reach their destinations, but after today, he'd give some serious thought to alternate means of transportation. Better yet, he'd be sure to schedule all future excursions for the summer.

Alex originally planned to leave on this archeological dig before Christmas, but his father had suffered a massive heart attack, prompting him to postpone his departure. Despite the marvels of modern medicine, the coronary damage was irreversible and William Innes died the day after Thanksgiving. Unable to bear the thought of his mother being alone over the holidays, aimlessly prattling about in the home she'd shared with her husband of thirty-four years, he'd invited her to come along on his trip. But she refused to be a burden. And as the plane pitched sharply to the right, this was one time he was thankful for her stubbornness.

After doing as the flight attendant requested, Alex braced himself for landing. The plane bounced and shook violently as it hit yet another updraft caused by the storm.

"This is your captain speaking. We've begun our descent, ladies and gentlemen, and I have the runway lights in view. We should be landing in the next few minutes," the pilot announced.

Alex released the breath he'd been holding, relieved to know they'd soon be on solid ground.

"Holy Crap!" Someone in the cockpit shouted. "We're losing speed and altitude too quickly. Try to pull her up or we will miss the runway."

"The thrust readings are off. Are you sure the pneumatic de-icing boots deployed properly?" another crewmember asked. "*Shite* man, you forgot to turn off the crew-to-passenger intercom." Those words were followed by silence.

Alex's knuckles blanched white from gripping the back of the seat in front of him, and as the old saying went, his life flashed before his eyes. While he was not a pilot, he'd seen enough television documentaries on plane mishaps to know that a significant build of ice on any surface of the plane, especially the wings, could interfere with the airflow and cause a plane to lose speed and stall. If the propeller blades, probes and windscreens were not kept clear of ice, or the engine intakes were blocked, it could result in a crash.

The de-icing boots were rubberized membranes installed on the wings and stabilizer control surfaces. In the event of an ice buildup, they were inflated with compressed air to break the ice, then returned the wing to the correct shape once deflated. He prayed they'd not failed.

Hope faded when the plane suddenly slanted sharply to the left and began a rapid decent. Amidst the terrified screams echoing throughout the cabin, Alex squeezed his eyes shut and began reciting the Lord's Prayer. But before he could finish, the aircraft hit the ground, then rolled to the side—the left wing snapping off upon impact. Sharp pain lanced across his forehead, then everything went black.

~ * ~

Confused and disoriented, Alex struggled to regain consciousness. He had no idea how long it had been since the plane crashed, but he was thankful to be alive. He inhaled slowly, his chest tightening with pain. Acrid smoke stung his eyes and the pungent odor of jet fuel assaulted his nostrils. He was suspended upside-down and the overstretched lap belt was the only thing holding him in his seat. He glanced to his left at the spot where the elderly couple once sat, but a gaping hole in the fuselage was all that remained.

He made the sign of the cross, hoping they might still be alive, but if not, he prayed their deaths were quick and painless. Alex groaned, touched his forehead and felt something warm and sticky beneath his fingertips. When he withdrew his hand, he saw blood.

Thoughts racing, he wondered if anyone else had

survived. Could he be of some assistance in getting people out of the plane who needed tending? He'd do what he could to help, but needed to free himself from the seat first. He reached for the seatbelt clasp, but hesitated when he saw a figure moving toward him, crawling on hands and knees though the smoky haze.

"Can anyone hear me?" the woman called out, then began to cough and sputter.

"I'm here," Alex shouted, then narrowed his gaze, trying to make out a face.

"Are you injured, sir?" the flight attendant asked. "Let me help you out of the seatbelt." She quickly released the clasp and, before he knew it, Alex dropped to ground with a thud.

"I've some cuts and bruises, but other than that, I think I'm fine." Unnerved by the eerie silence surrounding him, Alex grasped her by the shoulders. "Is anyone else alive or in need of help?"

"Let the crew worry about the other passengers, sir. You must leave the plane as quickly as you can." She pointed to the door marked emergency exit. "Go now. And once you're outside, someone will tell you what to do."

With no medical training to speak of, other than a basic first aid course and CPR, Alex agreed he'd be more of a hindrance than help if he stayed. Perhaps there was something he could do for his fellow passengers once he left the plane. He crawled to the exit and reached for the latch. But the door was wedged tight and wouldn't budge. Using his shoulder and as much strength as he could muster, he shoved until the metal gave way, and he tumbled out of the plane head first, landing in a pile of snow. He lay there for a moment, thanked God for letting him live, then slowly climbed to his feet.

He surveyed the crash site, the reality and the severity of the situation hitting him hard. Bodies and debris were strewn about, amidst pieces of tangled wreckage. A fire crew hosed down an intact portion of the fuselage, dousing flames that licked along that section of the plane. Emergency personal scurried about, searching for survivors. Several EMTs raced right by, but paid Alex no mind. Not a surprise, since he was certain there were others who needed their help more than he did.

"Are you able to walk on your own?" someone asked.

Alex jumped, startled when a woman suddenly appeared beside him and rested her hand on his forearm. She wore a long hooded cloak, her face hidden from his view.

"I think so." Alex brought a hand to his brow. "I have a gash on my head, but it appears to have stopped bleeding. My ribs are sore, but other than a few bumps and bruises, I'm okay." He studied her for a moment. "Are you a nurse or EMT?"

"I'm a healer," she whispered softly, then pointed to a triage area that was set up on the outskirts of the crash site. "If you'll go over there, someone will take care of you."

"A healer? Is that some fancy way of saying you are with the Emergency Evac Unit?"

"I dinna know what you mean. But it isna wise for you to stay here," she whispered, then held out her hand. "Come."

Alex took a step and stumbled, grateful when the woman grasped his upper arm to steady him. "I guess I'm not as ·stable on my feet as I'd thought. I hate to ask, but do you think you might help me over to the medical area?"

She lifted his right arm and draped it across her shoulder, then slid her left arm around his waist. "Lean on me." She took a couple of steps and paused. "Are you well enough to continue?"

"Yep. And I appreciate your help." Alex tightened his grasp on her shoulder and hobbled toward the paramedic station. When they arrived, she eased him onto a chair.

"Wait here. Someone will assist you in a few minutes

and tell you where to go." She patted his hand.

This time when she touched him, a strange spark of energy radiated from her fingertips. Soothing warmth crept up his arm, his pulse quickened, and he suddenly found it hard to breathe. When she lowered the hood of her cloak and smiled at him, his heart did a quick flip. She was not only stunning, but there was something familiar about her that he could not put his finger on. If he didn't know better, he'd swear they'd met before. But that was impossible. He'd never been here before. "I'm Alex Innes." He offered his hand to her. "I never caught your name."

"Innes, you say?" She frowned, then turned to leave. "I must be away."

"Wait." He stood and cupped her shoulder. "You can't just go without at least telling me who you are. Maybe when this is all over I could take you out to dinner as a show of my appreciation for your help."

She shrugged out of his grasp and faced him. "Out to dinner? I have no idea what you're havering about." A puzzled expression crossed her face as she backed away.

"Name your favorite restaurant and I'll take you there. I want to say thanks." Alex lied. While he honestly was appreciative, he couldn't shake the feeling he knew this woman. And if not, he'd really like a chance to get acquainted.

She shook her head and raised the hood of her cloak. "There is no need for you to thank me." She plodded through the snow toward the plane, then paused and glanced over her shoulder. "Ciara Dunmore," she said, then disappeared into the darkness.

Chapter Two

Alex shivered and wrapped his arms around his waist, trying to conserve a bit of warmth. He hoped Ciara might return, but his wish went unanswered. After waiting at least fifteen minutes for someone to come and tend to his injuries, he decided to make his way to the terminal instead. There were other passengers who needed attention far more than he did, and if he sat here much longer, he might freeze to death—an ironic turn of events, given he'd just walked away from a plane crash.

He rose to a wobbly stance, braced his aching ribs with his forearm, and sucked in a slow, deep breath. The terminal lights flickered in the distance and if he managed to remain focused and upright, Alex was confident he could make it there on his own.

Snow continued to fall, the drifts getting deeper by the minute, making it difficult to walk. But the thought of a warm place to sit and a piping hot cup of coffee kept him motivated. He trudged onward. As the door of the terminal came into view, he quickened his pace.

Alex staggered into the airport lobby, relieved he'd made it there under his own steam. He clung to the doorframe, taking a moment to catch his breath, the warmth of being indoors enveloping him. When he recognized a large group of passengers from the ill-fated flight standing off to one side, his heart leapt with joy. He was thrilled to see so many people had survived, but couldn't help wondering why there were no emergency personnel tending to the injured, no blankets, no coffee, nothing to offer them comfort.

"Please get in the line, sir," a woman holding a clipboard said as she came up behind him.

"I beg your pardon?" Alex whipped around, uncertain if

he'd heard her correctly. It stood to reason the airline would have some sort of protocol in place in the event of a crash, and he wanted to cooperate in any way he could. But after their near brush with death, he was shocked to learn that rather than seeing to their needs, the airport staff were asking the survivors to wait in a line.

"You need to join the other, sir. With so many souls involved, we must do this in a calm and efficient manner." She pointed to the group. "Your information will be taken in turn. We appreciate your patience."

When Alex noticed the elderly couple who'd been seated next to him on the plane, standing near the front of the line, he heaved a sigh of relief. He was happy to learn they too had survived and wanted to go to them. "If you'll excuse me, there are some people I need to speak to." He started toward Angus and his wife, but the woman scooted in front of him.

"I'm sorry, sir, but you must wait your turn. Once you've been processed, you'll be free to move on," she said sternly.

Stunned by the woman's lack of empathy, he tamped down the urge to tell her what he thought of her insensitive attitude. He was usually easy going and cooperative in the face of an emergency, but he was tired, cold, and in need of medical attention. Above all that, he had to let his mother know he was alive and put her mind at ease. Patience was not his strong suit right now, but he did his best to keep his frustration under control.

"I know you're just doing your job, and I'm sure you have rules to follow after a crash. However—" he began, but paused mid-sentence when he thought he saw Ciara walk by the window. He immediately turned and darted for the door, hoping to talk to her.

"You canna leave, sir. You must wait to be processed. A large man wearing the uniform of a security guard blocked the doorway. "Return to your place line."

"Please get out of my way. I have to talk to someone. It's important." Alex pointed out the window. "She just walked by and if I hurry I might be able to catch her."

Frowning, the guard crossed his arms over his chest and widened his stance. "That's an open field, not to mention a restricted area. There are no unauthorized personnel allowed out there. You need to go and wait with the others."

Anger tugged at Alex's gut. He was a passenger not a prisoner. If he didn't catch Ciara now, he might never have another chance. But it was obvious the guard wasn't going to budge from the doorway. Instead of trying to reason with the man, Alex moved to the window, peering into the darkness. There was no sign of Ciara and the snow outside was unmarred by footprints. He shook his head and dragged his fingers through his hair. He'd have sworn he saw her. But, perhaps it had been wishful thinking and not real after all. Maybe none of this was real and he'd wake up in his Manhattan apartment to find out he'd been dreaming.

"Is there a problem?" the woman tending to the line asked.

"Yes. I met a young woman on the runway right after the crash and was almost certain I saw her again a few minutes ago. She said her name was Ciara Dunmore. Do you know where I can find her?"

The woman studied her clipboard, then glanced up at Alex and shrugged. "I see no one by that name. Was she a passenger?"

"I believe she was with the emergency rescue team." Alex replied.

The woman placed her hand on his forearm. "This list is only for the passengers. I'm afraid I canna help you find the lass you seek. Please wait here and we'll process your information as quickly as possible. After which, you can be on your way."

"What about my luggage and access to a phone?" Alex

began to pace. "Everything I brought with me was in the baggage compartment of the plane, or what's left of it. And my mother will be beside herself with worry when she hears about the crash. I need to get in touch with her, but I lost my cell phone when I climbed out of the wreckage."

"Please try to remain calm. Those things will all be addressed in a timely manner, Mr. Innes. As I said, if you will just be patient, everything will be taken care of."

Alex glared at the woman. "How do you know who I am? I never told you my name."

"Why it is right here." She showed him the clipboard, placed her finger on his name, and read aloud. "Alexander Innes, seat 35 row G.

"That may be my name and where I was seated, but I need to talk to someone who can answer my questions and address my concerns." Frustrated, Alex stepped away from the others.

"Please, Mr. Innes, you must wait your turn."

Alex threw his hands in the air and marched toward a man he spotted in a booth near the arrival and departure desk. He had to get in touch with his mother immediately. And if he needed to buy new clothes and personal items, so be it. "You, there. I need some assistance." He waved at the man as he approached the rental car kiosk.

"What can I do for you, sir?"

Alex sucked in a deep breath as he read the man's nametag. "I need a phone and a car, Mr. MacDonald." He planted his hands on the desk and leaned forward. "*Please.*"

"I'm afraid that willna be possible. The phone service is down because of the storm and I couldna possibly give you a car." He pointed to the lineup. "If you wait your turn, someone will see to all your needs."

"I wish people would stop saying that." Alex counted to ten then addressed the clerk again. "I need to get in touch with my mother in Connecticut and let her know I'm alive.

My father died recently and I'm all the family she has left. The news of the crash could kill her. I'm also expected in Burghead this evening. My secretary made arrangements for a vehicle to be ready and waiting upon my arrival at least two weeks before I left New York."

"I understand that, sir. But the storm has closed many of the roads between here and Burghead," MacDonald replied. "Perhaps you would like to speak to my manager."

"I don't want to speak to your boss. I want a car." Alex pointed to his name on a list of rentals. "It says there that a blue, 2015, Ford SUV has been reserved in my name, and has already been charged to my credit card. Is it in the parking lot?"

MacDonald offered a hesitant nod. "Aye, but—"

Alex didn't give MacDonald a chance to finish. He rounded the counter and snatched the set of keys assigned to the designated vehicle from a rack on the wall, and hurried toward the door. If no one could help him find a phone, he'd find one himself. Even if he had to leave the airport to do so. "You have my name, information, a copy of my driver's license, and the payment has been made. If you have any other questions contact Ms. Leona Miller in the Archeology Department at State University in New York. She'll see that any further costs are covered. I'll return the SUV in three weeks, before I depart for the States."

When Alex opened the door of the terminal, he was greeted by a blast of cold air. He buttoned his jacket, turned up the collar, and tucked his hands into his pockets before heading toward the rental lot. Locating the SUV was easy, given there were only five vehicles left and four were compact cars. Wasting no time, he jammed the keys into the lock, opened the door, and climbed inside.

He winced when he fastened the seatbelt across his chest, his ribs still tender. Once he'd checked in at the dig site in Burghead and called to reassure his mother he was alive, he'd stop by the emergency room and have them checked, along with the gash on his forehead.

After programming his destination into the GPS of the SUV, he pulled out of the lot and followed the instructions. Driving on the opposite side of the road proved to be a challenge at first, but one he was determined to master.

Several miles down the road, he began to regret his decision to leave the airport before the storm ended. Whiteout conditions made visibility next to nil and a strong north wind made steering difficult. If not for the vehicle's four-wheel drive, he'd have been stranded in one of the many drifts covering the road before he got far from the terminal's parking lot.

Alex tightened his grip on the steering wheel and squinted, trying to see through the snow and to remain on the highway. "Concentrate," he muttered, but was forced to swerve when he saw an old woman standing on the road in front of him.

Hitting a patch of black ice, the SUV skidded and did a complete circle before coming to rest in a huge snow bank. He threw the gearshift into reverse and tried to back up, but his wheels spun and vehicle didn't move. He cursed and tried again, but to no avail. Could his luck get any worse?

Resigned to his fate—he was not going anywhere until morning—he climbed out of the SUV and slammed the door. The old woman came to mind. What was she doing in the road, and was she injured or safe? He surveyed the area, but his search for the woman came up empty. Perhaps he'd hit his head harder than he realized during the plane crash and had imagined the whole thing. He touched his brow, surprised when he felt no cut or bump.

Frigid wind cut through him like a knife, stealing his breath. His toes were numb and his ears, hands, and face were nearly frozen. Dressed in light clothing, he suspected he'd die of hypothermia before a tow truck could come for him. The roads were deserted, so the likelihood of getting picked up by a passing motorist was slim-to-none. He set out on foot, hoping to find a croft and Good Samaritan who might grant him sanctuary.

"This night isna fit for man nor beast," a woman said.

Alex spun around, looking in all directions, but saw no one. "Who's out there? Show yourself."

An old woman dressed in a long dark cloak stepped out of the shadows. "You dinna have to shout. A simple request will suffice."

Alex jumped. "You startled me. What in the hell are you doing out wandering the woods in the middle of a blizzard? Better yet, why were you standing on the road? You could have been killed and so could I."

"I was in no danger," she replied simply. "You on-the-other-hand, must get out of this inclement weather or you will catch your death of cold and perish. I'd suggest you go back from whence you came." She turned to leave.

"That would be easier said than done." He didn't bother to hide the sarcasm in his tone. "After swerving to miss you, I buried my SUV in a snow bank. I'm not going anywhere until morning when I can get a tow truck to pull me out."

"I have a croft not far from here. If you wish, you may wait out the storm there. But when the sun rises, it would be best if you returned to your home across the ocean."

The old woman headed into the woods, but Alex darted in front of her, blocking the way. "How did you know I came from America?"

"Is that what they call it?" She shrugged. "One only needs to listen to the way you speak to know you are na from Scotland. If you wish to get out of the cold, clear the way and you may accompany me. If na, I will go on without you. The choice is yours."

She stared at him with such intensity, the hairs on the back of his neck bristled. He didn't know what to make of the woman or if he could trust her, but she was right about one thing. If he didn't get out of the cold, he'd not make it until tomorrow. He stepped aside. "Lead the way."

They traveled a short distance in silence, arriving at a small hut nestled in the woods. "You live way out here, *alone*?"

"Dinna sound so surprised. I may have seen many summers, but I am quite capable of fending for myself." She shoved open the door and entered. "No one dares bother me."

Alex followed, a welcome waft of warm air, scented with a hint of peat enveloping him. He moved to the hearth and held his hands over the flames. "Ah, that feels wonderful."

"Perhaps you would like to take off your boots. You're dripping water all over the floor," she scolded.

"Sorry." Alex retuned to the door and kicked off his boots. He glanced around the croft—a simple, one-room dwelling that looked more like a throwback to the twelfth century than a modern day house.

"Are you hungry?" The old woman hunched over a caldron, stirring the contents. "I have some broth simmering. It will warm you from the inside out." She filled a wooden bowl and handed it to him, along with what looked like a slice of bread. "I made the bannock this morning and there is honey in the crock on the table. You look like you could use a hearty meal."

"Thanks. It smells great." Alex placed his bowl on the table, then pulled up a stool and sat. He dunked the bannock in the steaming liquid before popping it into his mouth. "You don't have many modern amenities. I guess it would be useless to ask if you have a phone."

She grinned at Alex, revealing a crooked set of teeth. "I have what I need."

"A phone?" Alex asked.

She shook her head. "I dinna know what you are talking

about, but what you see is what I have. There are some pelts on the shelf by the hearth and you are welcome to make a pallet on the floor. In the morning, I expect you to return to your home in this *America* you spoke of."

"I won't be going home right away. I'm an archeologist and am here to examine some ancient artifacts and the bull stones that were unearthed at the old Pict fort in Burghead earlier this summer."

The old woman narrowed her gaze and wagged a boney finger at him. "One shouldna disturb the past or meddle in things that are na your affairs. I insist you leave Scotland on the morrow and dinna return."

"I hate to disappoint you, but I have no intention of leaving before my work here is done."

The woman placed a mug containing a pungent smelling liquid in front of him. "Drink this tea. It will help you sleep."

He sniffed the brew and screwed up his nose. "What's in this?" He shoved the drink across the table. "I think I'll pass."

Her pleasant expression darkened. "Do you refuse my hospitality?" She slid the mug closer. "Is this how you repay my kindness?"

Not wanting to appear rude or ungrateful, Alex picked up the mug and took a sip—something he quickly regretted. The brew tasted as foul as it smelled.

The woman watched until Alex drained the mug. "Now you've finished, it is time to sleep."

Alex rose and the room suddenly began to spin. He took a step and stumbled, using the back of a chair to steady himself. "What was in that brew?" He staggered toward the hearth, grappling for the mantel in order to remain upright. "I don't feel so good," he groaned and slid his hand over his stomach. Had she poisoned him?

"It will help you to sleep." The woman laid a pelt on the floor and pointed to it. "Rest now and in the morning you will be ready to begin your journey home."

"I told you I'm not leaving." His words slurred and, unable to remain standing any longer, Alex dropped to his knees. He peered up at her and gasped when he realized the pleasant, cherub-faced elderly woman who'd welcomed him into her home no longer stood before him. In her place was a hunchbacked old hag with weathered skin and stringy white hair. "Who are you?"

"They call me Cailleach. And you will go back where you came from or suffer the consequences."

Alex immediately recognized the mythical name. He recalled the legends behind the Celtic fire festival of Imbolc, which fell on the second of February, halfway between the Winter Solstice and Spring Equinox, in an attempt to appease the evil hag who held the country in winter. The ancients believed that Brigid, the virgin fire goddess and keeper of the living flame and sacred wells containing the waters of life, spread a mantle of green across the land, prompting the growth of the first flowers of spring.

But it was just that, a myth. He tried to speak but he couldn't form the words. He tried to focus, but his vision blurred and he collapsed on the floor. Helpless as a new babe, he stared at the flames flickering on the hearth, shocked when Ciara's beautiful face flashed before his eyes. Her arms outstretched, she begged for his help. Alex reached out to her, but the image faded, as did the light.

Chapter Three

Nausea twisted Alex's gut and his head pounded. He groaned and brought his hand to his brow. He was not much of a drinker, but given his current hangover, he must have really tied one on last night. If only he could remember.

He languorously stretched, then glanced around the room, sitting up with a start when he realized he was lying on a moth-eaten pelt, tossed on the floor of an ancient croft and not atop the king-sized bed in his Manhattan loft. Dizzy from the sudden move, his stomach did a quick flip and he swallowed hard against the bile rising in his throat. But when he gazed into the flames of a low-burning fire on the hearth and once again saw the image a beautiful young woman reaching out to him, he rubbed his eyes in disbelief, certain he had lost his mind.

"Please help me, Alex. Only you can save me from Cailleach and free us from winter." He swore he'd heard her speak to him.

"Ciara?" Alex muttered, then gave his head a rough shake as the vision faded and memories of the plane crash, the storm, and the old hag came back to him. Cailleach had warned if he didn't return to the States as she demanded, he'd suffer the consequences. Did she mean the loss of his senses and grip on reality?

His mother came to mind and his heart clenched. By now she'd heard about the crash and was grieving the loss of her only son. Getting to Burghead and phoning to put her mind at ease was even more important now than ever.

Once his head stopped spinning and his stomach settled, Alex rose, went to the window, and peered outside. Rays of sunlight warmed his cheeks. And while the ground was covered with at least two feet of fresh snow, the storm was over and there wasn't a cloud in sight.

After another quick scan of the croft to make certain the hag was not around, Alex decided it was the perfect time for him to leave. He grabbed his jacket and patted the breast pocket, relieved the amulet was still there. Wasting no time, he slipped his arms into the sleeves, tugged on his boots, and stepped outside, greeted by a blast of cold, crisp air.

The SUV was buried in a snow bank not far from the croft, but Alex wasn't sure where. He turned full circle, surveying the area, then scratched his head. Snow was falling so heavily when he arrived, he had no idea from which direction he'd come. If he wandered off in the wrong way, he could get lost.

He lifted the collar of his jacket and jammed his hands into his pockets. If he didn't start moving soon, he'd freeze where he stood. When he spotted a horse tethered to a lean-to behind the croft, he approached the mare with his hand outstretched. He hadn't ridden since he was a boy, but he'd always heard that once you learned, you never forgot.

"Easy, girl," Alex cooed and stroked the horse's mane. "I only mean to borrow you. Once I've reached Burghead, I'll see you're returned to your owner." He spotted an old blanket hanging over a fence rail and laid it across the mare's back before climbing atop the beast. Riding without a proper saddle was a new experience, but nothing about this trip had been normal. He pressed his heels into the animal's sides and she lunged forward.

He hung on for dear life, relieved when the horse finally slowed to a walk. Using the sun's position in the sky to guide him, Alex headed north, but as he neared what appeared to be the seaside town he sought, he reined in his mount, stunned to spot what appeared to be a medieval village and a castle in the distance.

"Alex," a man shouted, then rode up beside him. "Where the devil have you been, cousin? Your da was beside himself with worry, na to mention furious. You disappeared well over a fortnight ago without telling anyone where you were going or when you'd be back." He spoke in an ancient Gaelic tongue.

Stunned, Alex stared at the stranger, his mouth gaping open. He had no idea who this man was or how he knew his name, but he understood everything he said.

A renowned history professor, his paternal grandfather spoke fluent Gaelic, and insisted Alex learn the language of his ancestors as soon as he was old enough to talk. Today he was thankful for that gift.

The man crossed his arms over his broad chest and returned Alex's stare. "Care to tell me where you've been? Your da thought mayhap you'd been captured by one of his enemies." His brow furrowed as he studied Alex. "What are these strange garments you are wearing?"

"What am I wearing?" Alex replied in Gaelic, equally baffled by the stranger's attire. The man wore trews, leather boots, a saffron tunic, and a heavy woolen cloak lined with rabbit fur draped about his shoulders. But what really caught Alex's eye was the baldric slung across his back and the sword at his side.

He'd seen pictures of the attire worn by Highlanders in the early twelfth century and had examined countless artifacts from the time period, but this was different. The man was actually wearing the authentic garb. "Is there some sort of re-enactment going on?" Alex finally asked in English, having no idea how to say the word in Gaelic?

"What?" The man cocked his head and glared back. "You're dressed oddly and acting very strange, cousin. First you speak in Gaelic and then in some strange tongue. Have you gone daft, and where did you get that nag?"

Bombarded with questions, Alex scrubbed his beard-stubbled chin. "I—I borrowed the horse," he replied in halting ancient Gaelic. How could the man speak ancient

Gaelic and not English? It was impossible to find anyone in modern Scotland who could understand Gaelic but not English. Ancient Gaelic. Twelfth century clothing and weaponry. The hag's primitive cottage. He couldn't quite believe it, but the only explanation was that somehow he had travelled to the twelfth century. What was happening to him? He returned the man's stare, deciding it might be best to learn a little more about his situation before saying any more.

Regarding Alex curiously for a moment more, the man finally shrugged. "Come then. I'll race you back to the Castle. Mayhap some of your da's whisky will loosen your tongue and refresh your memory. But best have a good excuse for being away for so long." The man dug in his heels and his horse bolted toward the curtain wall.

Alex blinked several times in disbelief at the stone structure on the horizon, and beyond to the Pict fort. If his facts were correct, the stronghold, once belonging to his ancestors, had fallen into ruins centuries ago, right after the collapse of the feudal clan system in the Highlands. And what was left of the fort lay buried beneath modern day subdivision—except for a small section of unearthed ramparts, the site of their dig, and the sacred Burghead well.

He raked his fingers through his hair. None of this made any sense. Was he dreaming or had he truly lost his mind? He was a man of science. It was physically impossible for a person to go back in time, yet somehow he appeared to have done it. Maybe he had died in the plane crash and this was what heaven was like for an archeologist. Uncertain how long this fantasy would last, and convinced the answer might lay beyond the castle walls, he followed, overtaking the man as they reached the portcullis.

Chains clanged and iron groaned as the large metal bars rose, granting them entry. They rode side-by-side until they reached the steps of the castle, then the other man dismounted and handed his reins to a young lad. "Stable my horse and take care of Lord Alex's mount as well."

"Aye, Lord Blair." The lad peered up at Alex and smiled. "I'd be pleased to care for your mount, m'lord. Is she new?"

Blair. At least he had a name by which to refer to the man who called him cousin. Now he had to come up with an explanation about his horse. He nodded and addressed the lad. "My mount stumbled and fell, injuring its leg, so I borrowed this one."

"You must have hit your head as well. That would explain your odd behavior," Blair said as he trotted up the castle steps.

Alex dismounted and handed over his reins. "Thank you—"

"David, m'lord."

"Thank you, David." Alex tousled the boy's hair.

"Are you coming?" Blair called out from atop the steps. "Or do you forget where you live as well?" He tossed back his head and laughed. "Your da will be glad to see you're hale and hearty."

"I'm coming." Alex slowly climbed the stairs, his gaze darting around the bailey of the castle, in reverent awe of everything he saw.

Upon entering the castle, Alex halted, his mouth again dropping open in utter surprise. Once the initial shock was over, he fought hard to contain his excitement. He smiled, imagining this must be how a kid would feel if he were set free in a room full of candy and ice cream. He didn't know where to look first.

Servants, dressed in the attire from the twelfth century, scurried about the main floor of the structure. Armed warriors warmed themselves by a large stone hearth, above which hung the Clan Innes crest. His gaze darted from the medieval furnishings to the brightly colored tapestries adorning the walls. If only he had his cell phone so he could take some pictures. No one in their right mind was ever going to believe him when he told this tale. Hell, he wasn't sure he believed it himself.

Blair gave him a shove. "Are you going to go and see your da right away, or do you plan to stop by your chamber first and put on something proper?"

"My chamber," Alex mumbled as he continued to stare at his surroundings. "Lead the way."

Blair laughed and dashed up a set of stairs leading to the second floor. "You're really going to play this memory loss farce to the hilt." He led Alex down a long corridor, stopping when he came to an ornately carved door, which he opened. He bowed and ushered Alex in with a sweep of his arm. "Change and wash up. I'll find your father and tell him his prodigal son has returned." He left, closing the door behind him.

Alex surveyed the room. It was exactly how he'd pictured a typical medieval chamber would look. Or at least one belonging to a member of the laird's immediate family. A large bed and several pieces of carved furniture occupied the center of the room, and a fieldstone hearth took up one whole wall. On two of the walls hung colorful needlework and the last held every type of medieval weaponry imaginable. He could literally spend years in here, studying each artifact. And if stuck in the past for the rest of his days, he might do just that.

From a table beside the bed, he picked up a pewter goblet, admired the fine workmanship, then moved to a shelf containing several pairs of trews, tunics, stockings, and boots. A unique find, since the average man from that era would be lucky to own one of each. After selecting something more in tune with the time period, he quickly changed, then hid his jacket and the amulet beneath the mattress on the bed.

Now what do I do next? He wondered. A feast for his

eyes, there was so much to see. But he soon had his answer when a loud ruckus in the bailey caught his attention. He raced to the window, threw open the shutters, and peered outside. Below him in the inner courtyard, a crowd gathered around several burly warriors. They held someone prisoner. And if he wasn't mistaken, it was a woman. Her feet were hobbled with chains and ankle irons, shackles binding her wrists.

"None of my affair." He tried to convince himself, but he was drawn to the woman by a force he could not explain or deny. And when she raised her chin and the hood of her cloak fell back, he gasped. "Ciara," he mumbled under his breath.

He should go to her and demand they set her free was the first thought that sprang to mind. Then he laughed inwardly at this folly. Who was he to think the laird, or anyone for that matter, would listen to him, let alone set Ciara free? The laird would likely have him arrested, once he'd stop laughing at his demands.

His eyes fixed on her face, he searched his mind for answers. He couldn't just stand here doing nothing. But he had no feasible plan to save her either. There was no telling what they intended to do to Ciara, and he was one man against so many. Logic told him to stay out of it, but his heart told him to jump in with both feet.

They'd only met yesterday, yet she'd put herself in harm's way to help him on the runway, so he at least owed it to her to come to her aid now. Not his typical, organized way of handling things, he'd decide what to do, once he'd checked out the entire situation.

Alex ran until he arrived at the bailey, then elbowed his way through the throng of onlookers until he reached Blair and an imposing-looking man he guessed was the laird.

"You've done well, men. Take her to the well and see she is chained to the wall," the laird said. "I'll take no chances with her. The Imbolc festival is but two days hence and the winter hag will require her offering and nothing less."

"Wait. What's going on?" Alex doubled over at the waist, gasping for air. "What do you mean the winter hag will require her offering?" The words spilled out before he could stop himself.

Blair grabbed Alex by the upper arm and yanked him upright. "Hold your wheesht. Your da has spoken and willna take it well if you challenge his decision in front of the clan. She is the chosen one and there is naught you can do to change things."

If Alex didn't know better, he'd think the laird was referring to some sort of human sacrifice. He scratched his head. Maybe he'd misunderstood. If his calculations, based on what he'd seen, were correct, and he wasn't in the midst of a very vivid dream, he'd somehow wound up in the early eleven-hundreds. Human offerings were not only a barbaric pagan ritual, but they hadn't been practiced for centuries, not since birth of Christianity.

True, some of the ancient festivals still practiced in Christian Celtic society were rooted in pagan times. But to take a human life was just not done.

"Chosen for what?" Alex wrenched free of Blair's grasp. Hopefully he had misunderstood and Blair could clarify.

"You really did hit your head, didn't you?" Blair lowered his voice so only Alex could hear. "She is the maiden chosen as the offering to Cailleach. Imbolc will soon be upon us, the time when the herds come down from the hills and the lambs are born. A time when we watch for snakes emerging from their holes and pray for rain so Cailleach canna gather wood to fuel her fire. A time for the light to return and for new beginnings."

"I know what Imbolc is," Alex snapped. "But they can't seriously be thinking of holding this young woman prisoner in a cave? With the intention of sacrificing her?"

"As you are well aware, cousin, time is almost up and none of the sacred water needed to appease Cailleach remains. This has been a very harsh winter and the only way to ensure spring comes this year is for a virgin—an oldest daughter who is pure of heart and soul—to offer herself to the winter hag in return for spring. You know this to be true," Blair whispered.

"It's barbaric," Alex mumbled under his breath. To outwardly challenge these people's beliefs and ceremonies based on what he knew to be true historical facts would be a foolish act on his part. He wasn't certain whether he'd actually stepped back in time or not, but it felt very real. And if he was in their world, he must hold his tongue. Something told him there would be many thing that challenge his grip on reality, forcing him to suspend disbelief. At least for the time being.

"Have you something you wish to say, Alex?" The laird glared at him.

Alex had plenty to say, but was afraid if he started, he'd not be able to stop. Instead of commenting, he held his tongue and shook his head. Running off at the mouth about his personal beliefs and questioning the need for this ritual would not help Ciara.

The laird faced the crowd. "I have spoken and my word will be honored. The Dunmore lass will present herself to Cailleach in hopes that she will find her a suitable gift and exchange her life for spring." His proclamation completed, he turned his attention to Alex, his brow furrowed. "Now that I have dealt with the matter of the Imbolc offering, I demand an explanation."

"An explanation?" Alex chewed on his bottom lip. He had no doubt the laird had many questions to ask. *Who is this man pretending to be my son*, topping the list?

"You are aware of what was required this year, yet you

seem to have issue with it all of a sudden. Your speech is odd and you are behaving strangely," the laird snapped.

Blair stepped forward before his uncle finished. "He fell off his horse and bumped his head. I'm sure he'll be fine once he's had a chance to rest. And maybe had a tankard or two." He wiggled a brow and tried to make light of things. Hopefully easing the tension between father and son. "Come, cousin, let's leave this to your da and the clan elders. There are a couple of new tavern wenches I want you to meet."

Alex's gaze locked with Ciara's, pleading emerald eyes a man could get lost in. "I'm not going anywhere. Not until she's released."

"Then you will be waiting until Hell freezes over," the laird snapped, "because I certainly won't allow this land to remain frozen. Meet me in my chamber once we've finish here. And be prepared to explain your behavior of late." The laird faced the guards. "Take her to the well."

Alex watched as the warriors led her away. He couldn't help wondering why she didn't fight or beg for mercy. But then again, her stoic spirit and refusal to cower before her captors only added to her appeal, making him even more determined to get to know her better. But first, he had to rescue   her.

Chapter Four

"Take your hands off me." Ciara glared at the guard when he grabbed her elbow and tugged her toward the ancient Pictish Fort that was located at the edge of the village. She dug in her heels and refused to budge. "I'm capable of walking on my own. I dinna need or want your assistance."

"Your wants and needs dinna matter," the guard snapped.

"Is she causing a problem, Fergus? Throw her over your shoulder if you must, but let's get this over with," the second guard said.

"That willna be necessary." She tilted her chin. "Unhand me, and I will go with you."

"Suit yourself." Fergus released his grip and gave her a shove, causing her to stumble. "Dinna dally."

Ciara staggered, but managed to remain upright. "While I see no point in it, my ankles are in irons and my hands are bound with shackles. If you remove them, I could walk more quickly."

"And risk having you run off?" Fergus shook his head. "I think not." He yanked on the chain.

"I have no intention of running off. But even if I chose to run, it's na like I could get away from the two of you."

"The laird's orders," Fergus grunted.

"Move." The second guard planted his hand on Ciara's shoulder, steering her toward the fort that loomed before them. But when they reached their destination, they did not enter. Instead, they travelled along a tall grassy hill that formed one of the ramparts.

Fergus threw back his head and laughed when they arrived at the entrance to the well. "Your new home awaits, m'lady. At least until the winter hag decides if you suit her fancy. The bowels of the netherworld yawn before you."

Ciara stared the opening of the cave, a cold shiver skittering up her spine.

The second guard knelt beside her and unlocked the ankle irons.

"What do you think you're doing, Donald?" Fergus asked. "The laird will skin us alive if she gets away."

"It's either free up her feet so she can walk down the stairs, or carry her," Donald replied. "Unless you have a better idea, hold your *wheesht*."

"Get on with it, Donald." Fergus blew on his hands and rubbed them together. "The sooner she's down there and the hag comes for her, the better. This has been a brutal winter and I willna be sad to see it go."

Donald lifted Ciara's right foot, removed her slipper, and repeated the action with the left.

"What are you doing now?" demanded Fergus.

"She willna need these where she's going. And with the ground frozen and covered with snow, should she decide to run, she'll na get far if barefoot" He tossed the shoes to Fergus. "I'm na married, maybe your wife can use them."

Fergus tucked the slippers into his belt and grabbed the chain attached to the shackles binding Ciara's hands. "Let's go, lassie, and watch your step. We dinna want you to fall and crack open your skull. If you do, the laird will have to find another wench to give to Cailleach."

Her feet numbed by the cold ground, Ciara found it difficult to take a step, but she'd not beg for mercy, nor would she admit her weakness. She squared her shoulders and began her decent, mentally counting each of the twenty steep, stone steps leading to an enclosed chamber with rounded corners. In the center of the dark cavern was a spring-fed, rock-hewn basin, surrounded by a narrow ledge. She'd been there more than once to fetch the water for healing purposes and in preparation for the Imbolc festival in her nearby village. But now she entered the forbidden space as a prisoner. Her chest tightened as she stared into the darkness. She'd not be leaving this time.

Created not only for the purpose of drawing water, the well was the setting of religious and pagan ceremonies dating back to ancient times. Considered a place of worship, purification, and healing, the hot spring was also used by the former inhabitants of the area for executions by drowning.

When they reached the bottom of the stairs, she peered up at Fergus. "I forgive you. I know you believe this is for the best. But it wasn't necessary. I had every intention of offering myself."

As if frozen on the spot, Fergus stared down at her.

Donald placed his hand of Fergus's back and pushed, nearly knocking him off balance. "Let's get it over with. This place makes me nervous." He removed her cloak and set it on a nearby rock. "She'll na be needing this either."

Fergus offered a curt nod and lit a lit torch, using it to light the way as they entered the cavern. He inched along the narrow ledge with his back pressed against the wall, taking Ciara with him. When they came to a wider lip of stone, he halted. "This is far enough." After chaining her to iron rings attached to the wall. "May the Cailleach be pleased by your sacrifice, lass," he said as he left the cave.

Ciara closed her eyes and muttered a prayer as Fergus disappeared from view and she was shrouded by darkness.

~ * ~

Not allowing himself to intervene when the warriors led her away took every ounce of self-control Alex could muster. Heart hammering, his gut twisted in knots, he gritted his teeth and repeatedly opened and closed his clenched fists as he stared at the entrance to the fort.

His mind racing, Alex tried to regroup his thoughts. So

much had happened over the last twenty-four hours, he seriously questioned his sanity. He'd yet to determine why he'd suddenly found himself in the twelfth century, but he was convinced there was a reason he'd come to Scotland precisely when he did, why he'd been spared in the plane crash, and why this beguiling woman kept popping into his life. Now all he had to do was link the pieces of the puzzle together, and try to figure out why events that according to documented history would not have taken place during this era were not only happening, but were accepted by these people as necessary.

A wave of guilt washed over him. Was he a coward for not chasing after Ciara and fighting for her freedom? He'd never forgive himself if anything happened to her because he failed to act. But to do so in the presence of so many villagers and under the direct scrutiny of the laird and his warriors could have only ended in disaster. Before he could help her, he needed a plan. For it to be successful, he'd have to bide his time and not draw suspicion, regardless of how he felt about Ciara or her plight.

"That look of determination on your face can only mean one thing, cousin." Blair leaned closer. "If you're considering the idea of going against your da's wishes and setting the lass free, you'd best think long and hard about the consequences."

"Tell me, what you would do if in my place?" Alex glowered at Blair. "If she is left chained to the wall with no food or water, she'll die."

"First, I wouldna question the ritual. Our ancestors have appeased the winter hag since before the time of the Druids. Second, I wouldna deliberately invite your father's wrath for a woman you dinna know." Blair wriggled a brow and leaned closer. "Unless there is something you havena told me and wish to share. Mayhap a dalliance is the real reason you disappeared."

"You're spouting nonsense." Alex replied. "I'm aware

B.J. Scott

the ritual's important, but I refuse to stand by and allow Ciara or anyone else perish. Not when I can do something to stop it. And I could never live with myself if I let that happen. I understand the fear of being locking in winter forever, but there has to be another way."

"Get caught setting her free and you willna have to worry about that. If I dinna know better, I'd say you have a personal interest in this woman. Are you sure there is na something you want to share?"

"Nay." Alex answered.

Blair crossed his arms over his chest and widened his stance. "Then why is her life so important to you? She is a Dunmore. There has been enmity between our clans for centuries. In addition to that, she was caught trespassing on our land and dipping a bucket into the sacred well, claiming she needed the water to heal her ailing father. Your father feared she intended to try some dark magic in an attempt to save herself and he couldn't take that risk."

"She's a healer and not a witch." Alex countered sharply.

"How do you know she's a healer?" Blair challenged.

"I just know. And if she claims she needed the water badly enough to risk capture, then I believe her. It's no excuse to sentence her to death."

"This plan has been in place for years. We knew an offering would need to be made to the hag soon. It has never bothered you before. Drop this and come away with me, Alex, afore you do something you'll later regret."

"Well it bothers me now." Alex began to pace. And while Blair might think he'd he taken leave of his senses, nothing he could say was going to change Alex's mind. "I'm assuming the well will remain guarded." If he intended on helping Ciara, he needed a plan.

Blair's frowned as he studied Alex. "What sort of a question is that? You know as well as I that your da wouldna risk her changing her mind and bolting. Then again, her clan might decide to help her escape even if it would mean perpetual winter for them as well." He cupped Alex's shoulder and tried to steer him toward the bailey. "Forget this fool's errand and join me for a drink. Willing lassies and cold brew await."

Alex planted his feet and shrugged free of Blair's grasp. "I'll pass. I'm not thirsty and have no need for a dalliance with a wench I don't know. Time is wasting and there is no point in beating this dead horse any longer. But don't let me stop you from enjoying yourself." He hoped Blair could be trusted to hold his tongue.

"You're a thrawn arse," Blair snapped. "Not only are you going to anger your father, but by helping the lass, you are sentencing all of us to an endless, bitter winter."

"I know you don't understand this, but I'm certain it isn't necessary for her to give her life to ensure the return of spring. Think what you will but I'll do whatever it takes to save Ciara," Alex said and darted toward the castle. If he was going to rescue her, he needed to prepare himself.

Once inside the keep, Alex headed for the stairs, intent on going to his chamber, but was stopped by a passing servant.

"Your da wishes to see you. He's in the great hall, m'lord." The servant pointed down a long hallway on the main floor of the castle.

"Thank you for letting me know. I'll go see him at once." Alex waited for the servant to go on his way, then dashed up the steps. The laird would have to wait.

Upon entering his chamber, Alex approached the weapon- covered wall and lifted a claymore. While struggling to hold on to the massive piece, he marveled at the workmanship, and wondered how a man could carry such a heavy blade into battle, let alone wield it. He was not a violent man, and had never struck another person in anger.

But holding the medieval weapon felt surprisingly natural, like he'd done this before. Ciara needed him and there was no place like the present to learn. After swinging the massive blade a few times, he opted for a much lighter broadsword.

Alex quickly donned a padded gambeson and leather gauntlets. He'd promised his father to return the amulet to its original resting place and after he'd helped Ciara, he intended to do just that. He contemplated taking it with him, but decided it would be safer if he returned it to its hiding place. Should he fail in his attempt to free Ciara and was caught, he didn't want the gem to fall into the wrong hands, so he tucked it away for safekeeping. Armed with his sword and a dirk tucked in his boot, Alex left the castle in search of the well.

As he'd suspected the entrance was guarded by the same two warriors who'd taken Ciara away. Alex crouched in a large thicket of brush on the edge of the forest, close enough to the entrance of the well to assess the situation, but far enough away to remain unnoticed. After he'd rescued Ciara, he had no idea where he'd take her or how he'd keep her safe. But he'd worry about that once he'd subdued the guards and set her free. He prayed he was up to the task.

"One insurmountable problem at a time," Alex mumbled as he scanned his surroundings. He hated being so unprepared, but given the urgency of the situation, he'd have to do the best with what he had. Being alone and totally out of his element in the twelfth century didn't help either. He'd quickly discovered that studying the time period and actually being there in person were two totally different things.

He unsheathed the sword, not certain if the time came he could bring himself to use it. But he didn't see any other options. The guards were not about to hand Ciara over without a fight. He swung it up and over his head, getting a feel for it in his hand.

"Stand fast," a man said as he crept up from behind

Alex.

Chapter Five

Heart pounding, Alex whipped around to face the intruder, then rocked back on his heels and expelled the breath he was holding. "What in God's name are you doing here, Blair? You sacred the shit out of me."

"Better me than one of your da's warriors," Blair replied and squatted beside Alex. "While I'm convinced you're daft for attempting this fool thing, I thought you might need some help."

"Why are you risking your neck for me when you clearly do not agree with my decision to help Ciara?"

"Have I ever let you down in the past?" Blair asked.

"I can't honestly say that I've ever known you to abandon me." Even though he'd not met Blair until today, something told Alex that he could rely upon the man to watch his back. For a moment he considered disclosing the truth about being from the future, but it sounded unbelievable to his own ears, so he held his tongue.

"This is my idea, my fight," Alex continued. "I appreciate your help, but would rather you returned to the castle and forgot you saw me here." As the words left his lips, Alex wished he could take them back. While he didn't want Blair to risk the laird's wrath, he could really use the help of someone skilled with a sword by his side.

Blair shook his head. "Save your breath. You've always been more like a brother to me than a cousin. Where you go, I go. Even if I do think you're mad." Blair chuckled as he slapped Alex on the back, then peered through the bushes at the entrance to the well. "It willna be easy, but if we can distract the guards long enough to sneak up from behind, we might be able to subdue them."

"I won't ask you to risk your neck," Alex said. "If they

see our faces, they won't hesitate to report us to the laird."

"Then best we na get caught." Blair handed Alex a canvas sack and a length of rope.

Alex stared at the items. "What do you expect me to do with these?"

"If we wear hoods to cover our faces and dinna speak, the guards willna know who attacked them." He tugged a sack over his head and positioned the eyeholes, before securing it in place using the rope. "Unless we let them defeat us. And that is na going to happen."

The idea of losing caused Alex's stomach churn. If they were going to do this, he hoped Blair was as skillful as he was confident. "You're a stubborn fool, but we've obviously reached a stalemate, leaving me no choice but to let you assist me." Alex donned his hood and faced Blair. "How do you propose we distract the guards?"

Blair drew his sword. "You go to the end of the thicket and be ready to move when I give the signal," he explained. "I'll toss some rocks in the opposite direction to catch their attention. When they go to check out the cause of the disturbance, that's when we'll make our move."

Alex glanced at Blair's weapon, then slowly raised his own. "I hope you know what you're doing." He blew out a heavy sigh. "I have to warn you, I'm not sure how to wield one of these things." The words slipped out before he could stop them.

Blair tossed back his head and laughed. "This is na the time to jest, cousin. There is na a man in all of Burghead that could best you in a fight. Aside from me, perhaps."

"I was the state medium weight wrestling champ two years running when I was in college. But this is different," Alex mumbled aloud, his eyes locked on is sword as if in a trance.

"The state what?" A puzzled expression crossed Blair's face. "What on earth are you havering about?"

"Never mind. I was thinking aloud. But it's not important." Alex dismissed Blair with a wave of his hand and moved to the end of the thicket as instructed. "We'd better get this over and done while we have the chance." He parted the bushes, studying the two men guarding the entrance to the cave and swallowed hard. Not only were they huge, they were both heavily armed. "One problem at a time," he mumbled under his breath.

Blair scooped up a handful of rocks and hurled them across the open glen between the forest and the entrance to the well, the stones hitting the ground and catching the guards' attention immediately.

"Who goes there?" One of the men shouted and moved in the direction of the noise.

"Where are you going, Fergus?" one of the guards asked. "We were told na to leave our post."

Fergus pointed. "I heard a noise. Over there, Donald. Did you na hear it?"

Donald shook his head. "Nay and best you get back here before the laird finds out you're shirking your duty."

Blair tossed another handful of rocks, gaining Donald's interest as well.

"You see? I told you I heard something or someone." Fergus moved farther way from the cave entrance and Donald followed.

"Now!" Blair said as he rushed the men from behind.

Alex sucked in a deep breath for courage, quickly asked the Lord for strength, and followed with his weapon raised. But by the time he reached the guards, Blair had already made use of the element of surprise and struck both men across the back of the head with the hilt of his sword, knocking them out cold.

"Were you waiting for a formal invitation?" Blair grumbled as he sheathed his weapon. "Best you fetch the lass and make it fast. While I hit them hard, there is no telling when these buffoons will wake up. And when they do, they'll na be so easy to handle."

"What will you be doing while I fetch Ciara?" Alex saw no point in continuing the discussion of why he had not been of more help. He was just thankful he was not forced to injure or kill anyone.

"I'll keep an eye on these two and watch for others. Once you've freed the lass and are away, I'll head back to the castle," Blair replied.

"You're not coming with us?"

Blair shook his head. "Nay. I'll go home so no one is the wiser. Someone needs to make excuses for your absence and distract your da while you make your escape. If anyone asks where you are, I will tell them you went hunting and should be back in a few days. By the time they realize it was you who absconded with the lass, you'll be many miles from here and safe. Your da willna be happy when he finds out you're gone again, but he'll get over it once you return."

"What about the guards?" Alex asked as he nudged one with the toe of his boot. "Are you certain they can't identify us? What if one or both of them die? You hit them pretty hard."

"While both will awaken with a headache, they will survive. I'm also confident they have no idea who attacked them." Blair planted his hand on Alex's shoulder and pointed to the opening of the cave. "Now go get the lass. If you keep yammering, this will all be for naught. When these *bampots* report that their prisoner has escaped, I will be at your da's side, acting shocked and claiming to have no idea who might have done the deed. And if asked, I'll be vouching for your whereabouts."

Alex removed his hood and handed it to Blair. "This might frighten her." He grabbed a torch from a sconce on the wall and entered the cave, peering into the darkness. The space surrounding the pit was so small, he quickly located

Ciara. With his back pressed against the wall, he inched along the ledge until he reached the spot where she was shackled to the wall.

"Who are you and why are you here?" Ciara asked, a hint of fear detectible in her voice.

He raised the torch so she could see his face. "Alex Innes. I've come to free you." He unlocked and removed the iron cuff from around her right wrist, then quickly released the left. "There's not much time, so we must leave, *now*." He cupped her elbow, but she tugged free of his grasp.

"I canna go with you. You heard your father. I am the chosen one. This is my destiny." She lowered her gaze.

"I'm aware of that. But they mean to leave you here to die." He slid two fingers under her chin and lifted until their gazes met. She trembled at his touch, but didn't pull away. "Let me help you."

"You are the son of Laird Innes and I am nothing to you. I must do this. I have known that for years and so have you," she said. "Why do you care about what happens to someone from Clan Dunmore? There has never been anything but hatred between our families and it has only become worse over the last few years, as we drew closer to this."

His heart clenched when he noticed the unshed tears glistening in her eyes. "Perhaps the time has come for that animosity to end. It could start here and now, with you and me."

"What are you talking about? If I were to go with you, it would only make things worse for me and for my people. My clan would most likely be blamed for my escape and forced to face your father's wrath. And they'll take my sister instead. I'll na have that upon my head."

Alex couldn't believe she was refusing to accompany him, yet her unselfish bravery touched a spot deep within his soul. "Are you telling me you want to die, lass?" Alex asked and lightly stroked her cheek, catching a stray tear with his thumb.

"Of course I dinna *want* to die. I would much rather marry someday and raise a croft full of bairns. But I have no choice. I willna allow this to fall to my sister." She released a shudder breath. "I willna disgrace myself or my family."

"You could have your dream and more." He reached for her hand, but she took a step back. "Just come with me and together we will find a way for it to happen. I'll make sure the laird knows your clan had nothing to do with your escape."

"But my sister—"

"I won't allow her to be harmed."

"If only that were true, I would gladly accompany you. But how can you promise that? Someone must bear this burden and I was chosen. As much as I wish they would, so far the gods have revealed no other path"

He could sense by her tone that she was beginning to waiver. "And I can't leave you here to die. Please come with me." He didn't want to force her, but there wasn't time to argue. They had to leave before the guards woke up or anyone else came along. If she wouldn't go with him of her own accord, he'd have no choice but to carry her out. But hoped it wouldn't come to that.

"If only it were that simple. Imbolc is almost here. If Cailleach finds me a suitable offering, she will free the land from winter's icy grip," Ciara replied. "If angered, she may never allow the spring to come."

"I swear to you, spring will com. You are not responsible for appeasing the hag," Alex said. "And while I know everyone believes this Imbolc ceremony is critically important, I am confident that just as day turns to night—no matter what we do—spring will come whether you live or die."

"It is na for you to decide. If you interfere with your father's plans for me, he willna take it lightly," Ciara said. "I saw the way he glared at you and heard the anger in his voice when you questioned him earlier."

"You let me worry about the laird. I know he puts great stock in this, but it must be stopped. Have you ever known a day or night to go on forever?"

She shook her head. "Nay. But—"

He quickly closed the gap between them and placed his finger to her lips. "And you never will. It is the same with the seasons. Come with me. Choose life." As if drawn by a force to powerful to ignore, he leaned closer and brushed her lips with a gentle kiss. Pleased when she didn't resist him, he raised his head. "And to answer your question as to why do I help you? It's because I feel as if we have known each other forever, like we belong together." He clasped her hand. "You helped me after the plane crash. Let me help you, now."

"Plane crash?" Her brows knit together as she stared back at him. "What trickery is this? You speak in a strange tongue, and I have no idea what you're havering about." She tried to wrench free, but he held firm. "I've never heard tell of this place or thing you call *plane*. And we dinna know each other. We met for the first time today, when I was presented to your father in the bailey and na before."

Alex had no idea what to think of all this. He was certain she was the girl he saw. Furthermore, he absolutely knows the ritual isn't necessary. But he also knew arguing with her would get them nowhere and they had to act now. "There is no time to explain, but I will as soon as it is safe to do so. You must trust me." Alex tugged her toward him, the same spark of energy and surge of warmth he'd felt when she touched him at the crash site, radiating up his arm. Judging by her wide eyes and the blissful expression that crossed her face, she felt it too. "Please come with me, Ciara."

She hung her head. "Even if I did agree to go with you, the guards will never let us pass. How did you manage to get by them in the first place?"

"With a little help from a friend," Alex said, smiling. "The sentinels are currently incapacitated, but may not be for long. There really is no time to dally."

"You attacked them?" Ciara gasped and pressed a hand to her throat. They will surely report you to the laird, and he will no doubt hunt us down and punish you."

"You'd better hurry, cousin. No telling how long these buggers will be asleep," Blair shouted.

"We'll be right there," Alex answered, then looked at Ciara. "No need to fret." Alex squeezed her hand. "Every precaution was taken to see they don't know who attacked them. They can only tell the laird you're gone, not who helped you to escape."

"And you'll make certain my clan is na blamed and that my sister will be safe?" She nibbled on her lower lip.

"You have my word." He crossed his heart "Will you come with me?"

Her eyes lifted and she caught his gaze, then offered a hesitant nod. "Aye. I canna explain it, but I feel as if I can trust you."

"You can." Relieved he'd finally convinced Ciara to accompany him, he brought her hand to his lips and kissed the back of it. "Let's go. Mind your step, the ledge is slippery." Alex carefully led her toward the entrance. But as they emerged from the darkness, he noticed her feet were bare. "Where are your shoes?"

Ciara shielded her eyes from the bright sunlight. "The guards took them so I wouldna be able to run."

Blair rolled the larger of the two men over, then scooped the slippers from his belt. "Would these be them?"

Ciara nodded, then whispered to Alex. "Who is that man? Can he be trusted not to give you away?"

"Blair Innes, at your service, m'lady." He bowed before her, then handed her the slippers. "Best you put these on before your feet are frozen." He turned to Alex. "And you had best be off, cousin, before you're caught absconding with the lass and get thrown into the pit. I'll go back to the castle and cover for you as long as I can, but I doubt I can gain you much time, so hurry." He dashed off before Alex could respond.

"He's right," Alex said. "The longer we stay here, the better chance there is we'll be caught."

"Where will we go?" Ciara asked. "The laird will surely come after us, and we canna go back to my village. My clan wouldna welcome you, even if you did save me. They have no reason to trust you, and would surely turn you over to your da the first chance they got. Besides, that is the first place your da will look."

"He'll not find us there," Alex tried to reassure her. "I promised we wouldn't involve your clan."

"Perhaps, but if there is no one to exonerate them, I fear your father will wreak havoc on innocent women and bairns in retribution. It willna be the first time." Ciara hung her head. "Worse, he may choose another maiden to take my place. I couldna live with myself if another were to die in my stead. Perhaps this was a bad idea and I should go back."

Fearing she might bolt, Alex folded both her hands between his own. "I know the laird has been harsh on your people in the past, but he can be a fair man when he wants to be." He wasn't entirely convinced what he said was true, but knew if he waivered or gave her slightest indication that Laird Innes might retaliate against her clan, she'd insist on returning to the well.

"Are you certain? I havena seen that side of him, only the vengeful tyrant."

"Positive," he lied, but couldn't risk her going back. As soon as they were safe and Imbolc was over, he'd find a way to return to the castle for the talisman and convince the laird of the Dunmore clan's innocence. He prayed it wouldn't be too late.

We've come this far and must be away. I can't let you go back to the well. Nor can we stand here debating the pros and cons."

"The what?" Ciara stared at him. "You speak so oddly, m'lord."

"It means we can't waste time discussing all the good and bad reasons for leaving," Alex explained.

One of the guards groaned and tried to raise his head.

Being totally unfamiliar with the area, and having no idea where to take Ciara suddenly became the least of Alex's worries. They had to leave, *now*.

Chapter Six

Alex tugged on her hand. "Come on. We can hide amongst the trees and bushes, giving us a fighting chance to get away. There is no time to dally."

He dragged her through the woods, over fallen trees, dodging boulders, and across a frozen stream. They didn't stop running until her legs cramped and she couldn't take another step. Exhausted, she collapsed to her knees.

Alex squatted beside her. "I'm sorry for pushing you. I would have stopped sooner, but just as we reached the trees, I glanced over my shoulder and noticed one of the guards stagger to his feet. The more distance we put between us and them, the better."

Winded, Ciara rested her hands on her lap and sucked in a shallow gulp of air. She began to shiver, her teeth chattering. "I'm so cold, I can scarcely catch my breath." She glanced skyward. "And it is starting to snow, making it easier for them to follow us. This is madness" She wrapped her arms around her body in an attempt to stay warm, but in a lightweight gown and slippers there was not much hope.

"You're lips are turning blue." Alex caressed her cheek with his knuckle. "I was in such a damned hurry to get you out of the cave, I failed to notice you had no cloak. What happened to the one you were wearing when arrested?"

"They—they took it before chaining me up," she stammered. "They thought it would lessen my chance of running should I get away. And now we have, I'm afraid they made a wise decision."

"We need to find shelter. Do you have any idea where we can hide out?" Alex asked. He briskly rubbed he arms, hoping to generate some heat.

Ciara shook her head. "Nay, but you're right. We canna

stay here." As the words left her lips a strong sense of foreboding washed over her. "We must go so they canna track us."

"If it snows any harder, we won't have to worry about anyone following us. Our footprints will fill in as soon as we make them. But if we stay here talking, we will surely freeze to death. Can you stand?"

"Aye." She slowly climbed to her feet.

Alex quickly removed his padded gambeson and handed it to her. "Put this on. It might be too large, but it will help to keep you warmer than what you're wearing."

"What about you? If I take this, you'll have naught to keep you warm." She tried to hand the doublet back to him, but he refused to take it.

"Please, put it on. I'll be fine. I'm a lot sturdier than I look," he chuckled.

She knew he was as cold too, and only trying to be gallant, but he insisted she wear the gambeson and there was no point in arguing. Ciara slipped it on and nestled beneath the padded fabric—the garment still holding the warmth of his body. She inhaled deeply, his musky male scent made her head swim and caused her pulse to quicken. "This canna be," she muttered aloud.

"Is there something wrong?" Alex caressed her shoulder.

His touch made her tremble with forbidden delight. Overwhelmed by her powerful reaction, she glanced away, too embarrassed to look him in the eye. No man had ever elicited such responses. They were ones she'd only heard the women of her clan discuss in whispers. Was what he told her in the cave true? Had fate brought them together?

"If you're sure nothing is wrong, we best be on our way," Alex offered her his hand.

But she didn't accept. She gave her head a shake and trudged into the forest—the snow now past her ankles, making it difficult to walk.

As the storm intensified, Alex shielded his face against the wind and snow with his forearm. "We need to find a place to spend the night. The snow is not going to let up anytime soon. I can hardly see a few feet in front of us."

Ciara agreed, but remained silent. It took every bit of her concentration to remain upright and moving. Her feet were numb, as were her legs, the sting of the wind on her face unbearable at times. But they had to keep going. The farther from the castle they got, the better.

Alex clasped her arm and pointed to a light in the distance. "Do you see that croft over there?"

Squinting, she tried to focus, but her lashes were frozen and her vision blurred. "Nay, I canna see anything."

"Look closer." Alex cupped her head from behind and turned it slightly to the right. "Do you see it now? It's just beyond that hill."

"Aye."

"I wonder who it belongs to. Perhaps they will grant us shelter." He took her hand and moved in the direction of the croft. "But we must approach with caution."

Ciara planted her feet and refused to move. "What if they recognize us and turn us away. Or worse, hand us over to your father?"

"I understand your concerns, but it's a risk we must take. We can't go any farther in this storm." Alex replied. "The snow is damned near hip high in spots and every step is like a dozen normal ones. We're soaked to the skin and will die if we don't find shelter."

"Even if the owners of the hut turn out to be our foes?" She nibbled on her bottom lip and wrung her hands with worry.

"We have to take the chance and pray the occupants are friends. Can you make it?"

"I'll try," she stammered. But as she began to take a step, her legs buckled and she collapsed to her knees. She peered up at him. "You'll have to go on without me. I canna feel my feet and—"

Before she could finish, Alex scooped her up and carried her toward the croft, as if she weighed no more than a feather. Her heart fluttered and her stomach did a quick flip. She felt so safe and warm in his arms, as if it were where she belonged. Resting her head upon his chest, she focused on the hut, hoping whoever owned it would take pity on them and grant them entry.

~ * ~

Upon reaching the door, Alex knocked, but there was no answer. He peered in the window, and saw no one. "It looks to be deserted. Are you sure you don't know who owns this place?"

Ciara raised her head. "I dinna recall seeing this hut before. But the storm has me confused, so I canna be sure where we are, let alone who might live here."

Alex set Ciara on her feet as he tried the latch, relieved when he heard a click and the door swung open. After lifting her again, he entered the small dwelling, carried her to a stool before the hearth, and set her upon it. Puzzled, he glanced around the room. "There is no fire, yet they left a tallow candle burning. Had they not, I would never have noticed the hut amidst the trees."

"Perhaps they had to go outside to gather some wood and lost their way in the storm," Ciara said. "They could return at any minute."

"Well until they do, we are staying put." Alex found a pelt at the foot of the bed and wrapped it around her shoulders. "This should help to warm you. I noticed some wood in the corner by the hearth, so that couldn't have been the reason they left. I'll start a fire, and once it gets going, you can undress and I'll hang your things to dry."

Ciara gasped and pressed her hand to her heart. "Surely

you jest, m'lord. It wouldna be proper for me to disrobe when alone with a man to whom I am na wed."

Alex laughed. "Modesty should be the least of your worries. If you don't get out of those wet things, you'll catch your death of cold and it won't matter who sees you. Besides, you have the pelt to cover yourself and I promise to be a gentleman."

After placing several logs, some dry tinder and peat on the hearth, Alex used the lit candle to ignite the fire. He'd earned many merit badges when he was a boy scout, but wilderness survival was not one of them. He had no matches or lighter, so if he had to start a fire by striking stones or rubbing sticks together, they'd have been in for a very chilly night.

Alex watched as the flames rapidly consumed the dry wood, heat radiating from the glowing embers. "It won't take long for things to warm up." As he stood to address Ciara, a sudden flashback to the morning he'd awakened in the hag's croft invaded his thoughts. His gaze darted back to the hearth. But this time he didn't see Ciara's face in the fire. Alex swallowed hard against the lump of bile rising in his throat when the image of Cailleach appeared before him.

"I told you na to interfere in things that are none of your concern. Return the lass to the well and go back from where you came while there is still time. I'll na warn you again. Defy me and you will suffer the consequences."

"Is something amiss?" Ciara asked.

Alex stiffened, his gaze fixed on the image before him. The first time this happened he'd attributed the vision to an herb-induced stupor and an overactive imagination. But he was totally sober and there was no explaining what he now saw or heard. As the image began to fade, he whipped around to face Ciara. "Did you see that?"

She shrugged. "I see naught but the fire."

He glanced over his shoulder and the hag was gone. "I

must be more tired than I thought." Alex stirred the coals using an iron poker he found beside the hearth, then began a search of the hut, looking for a pot he could use to melt some snow. If Ciara was as thirsty as he was, he was certain she'd welcome something warm to drink.

"What are you searching for?" Ciara asked. She cuddled beneath the pelt, her teeth no longer chattering.

"An iron pot so I can heat some water. I'm also hoping to find some food we can eat. We could be holed up here for a while"

Alex found the idea of being stranded alone with Ciara more than appealing. He'd felt the overpowering attraction at the crash site, and it grew with each minute he spent in her company.

Never had a woman ignited such passion or desire, and he'd dated some beautiful, powerful women in his day. Perhaps that was it. Unlike the modern, ambitious, no-nonsense women he'd known, there was something pure and sweet about Ciara. He found her quiet, gentle demeanor, her inner strength and sense conviction refreshing as well as admirable. While she didn't outwardly exude confidence or pride in her appearance, he somehow knew those qualities existed without the need for fanfare or idle praise.

But there was so much more to this complicated situation than mere physical attraction. As determined as Alex was to save Ciara's life, Laird Innes and his warriors were determined to end it. These men were not driven by greed or ruthless brutality, but by something stronger, their beliefs.

The battle Alex waged wasn't just one between right and wrong, life and death, but against deep rooted tradition, honored by his ancestors for centuries. As barbaric as it sounded, Alex stood in awe of the influence the ancient superstition had on people's lives. He didn't agree with it, but he did respect its power.

If they were stranded here for days, he wouldn't mind. But the storm wouldn't last forever, and when it ended, their haven would no longer be a safe place to hide. With Imbolc less than a day away and given Ciara's part, the laird's men would be hot on their heels. They needed to find her and return her to the well in time for the ceremony to take place. Something Alex was determined to prevent from happening.

"Did you look over there?" Ciara pointed to a shelf near the window.

"I beg your pardon?"

"For the pot," she said smiling.

"Not yet, but I will." Alex moved to the shelf. "Jackpot!"

"I beg your pardon? What is jackpot?"

"It means I found what I was looking for." Alex held a black pot in the air so Ciara could see it, then checked inside several clay crocks. "We're in luck. There is some dried venison, some oats, and what looks and smells like mint. I'll melt some snow and add the mint. Then I'll make some porridge. It won't be anything fancy, but it will stick to—"

A noise outside the croft caught his attention. Alex fingered the hilt of his sword and swiftly moved toward the door. He brought a finger to his lips. "Shhh. And stay put. I think there might be someone outside," he whispered.

Ciara clutched the pelt beneath her chin, her eyes wide with fear. "Be careful, Alex. You dinna know who it might be."

"It could have been a fallen branch hitting the roof. It is windy and the croft is surrounded by trees," he said. "But if someone is out there, they know we're here. I've no choice but to find out." He sucked in a deep breath for courage, withdrew his sword, and reached for the latch. "Here goes nothing." Heart hammering, he yanked open the door, coming face to face with the last thing he expected.

Alex began to laugh. He slid his sword into its sheath, and glanced at Ciara.

She frowned. "What's so humorous?"

"This." Alex opened the door wider and motioned with a sweep of his hand. "The owner of the croft has a barrel of oats stored against the house and a buck decided to help himself."

Ciara smiled. "I'm glad it was a deer. For a moment I feared your father's warriors had found our hiding spot." With a downcast gaze, she nibbled on her lower lip. "How long do you think it will be before the storm ends and they come looking for us?"

"There is no way of knowing how long it will last, but judging by those dark clouds in the sky and the way it's coming down, I'd expect the storm will continue until tomorrow," he replied and went to fetch the pot. "As soon as it clears up enough for us to travel, we'll be on our way. For now, we need to rest up and stay warm." Alex once again headed for the door. "I'll scoop us some snow to melt. While I do that, why don't you slip out of your wet clothes and place them by the hearth. Wrap up in the pelt and when I return, I'll make us something to eat and drink."

Ciara offered a hesitant nod. "Hurry back."

Chapter Seven

"I doubt we'll have to worry about anyone tracking us." Alex entered the croft and shook off the snow. "It's coming down so heavily, you can't see two feet in front of you. I was thinking—" Alex began, but stopped midsentence when he noticed Ciara warming herself by the fire, her unbound hair a waist-length cascade of dark curls tumbling down her back. He swallowed hard, his gazed fixed on a vision of loveliness. She looked like an angel.

"I was . . . um." He tried to finish what he'd started to say, but found himself at a loss for words and unable to take his eyes off her.

"Is something amiss?" she asked, and turned to face him.

"No. Everything is fine."

While Alex was pleased to see she'd removed her clothing and hung them to dry as he'd suggested, she was not bundled up in the pelt. Instead, she stood before him in bare feet, wearing a white chemise that didn't quite come to her ankles.

"Where did you get the night gown?" He asked, almost choking on the words. The fabric of the garment was so thin he could make out the silhouette of each luscious curve of her slender figure, leaving little to his imagination.

"I found it in the wooden trunk at the foot of the bed. I hope the owner of the croft doesna mind." Ciara took the pot full of snow that Alex toted and suspended it from a chain hanging over the fire. "The coals are hot so it willna take long for this to boil."

"Yes. Hot," he replied, still dazed by her beauty. "You must be cold." He moved to the shelf beside the hearth, tugged down a length of plaid he'd noticed earlier, and returned to where Ciara stood. Doing his best to avert his eyes and to keep from staring with his mouth gaping open, he wrapped the wool fabric around her shoulders. He was only human, the temptation too great. "This should help to keep you warm."

"I'm sure it will. Thank you." Ciara smiled and touched his hand, a jolt of pure energy shooting up his arm and setting his heart afire.

"Are you certain there isna something bothering you? You look concerned or mayhap distracted." She lightly caressed his shoulder.

He *was* concerned, afraid she might get caught and sacrificed to the winter hag despite his efforts to save her. He worried about what would happen if he suddenly found himself back in 2017 without her. But right now, they were safe and together, so that was all that mattered.

"Everything is fine." Alex moved to the hearth, stirred the water as it began to bubble. "I don't know about you, but I'm starving," he said. Anything to keep his mind off of making love to her. "I'll make some porridge and we can have some of the dried venison I found earlier. It won't be fancy fare, but will do in a storm." He chuckled at his own joke, but Ciara didn't appear amused. "After we've eaten we'd better get some sleep. I have a feeling tomorrow will be a long and exhausting day."

Ciara wrapped her arms around her middle and stared at the fire. "What will become of us after the storm?"

"I thought since neither of us can return to our clans, maybe we could head toward Inverness after we ensure your sister's safety." Alex said. "We don't have to stay there. If you want, we can travel farther south once spring arrives, perhaps go as far as Edinburgh." Since he had no idea how long he'd remain in the past, he really had no right to make promises he might not be able to keep, but if he had Ciara in his life, he believed he could adjust to the twelfth century quite nicely.

"*If* spring arrives," she muttered.

Alex slid his arm around her waist and drew her against his chest. It was a gutsy, impulsive move on his part so he was glad she didn't try to push him away. "Of course the spring will come. I swear to you, it will come, and we have our whole lives ahead of us."

"I'm na so sure about that. And if the land is condemned to eternal winter, it will be all my fault." She tugged free of his embrace and began to pace. "I was the chosen one. It was my duty to offer myself to the winter hag so she'd release the land from her icy spell. But instead, in a moment of weakness, I ran away, shunned my duty, forsook my honor, and in doing so, I've risked my sister's life and disgraced myself before my clan." She stopped suddenly and whipped around to face Alex. "But it is still not too late for me to do what's right."

"What do you mean it's not too late?" he asked, even though he had a strong feeling he knew what she was about to say.

"If you were to take me back to Burghead and turn me over to your father, we could set the wrong to right," Ciara said. "You could tell him you found me wandering in the woods while you were hunting and brought me back so the Imbolc Ritual could be completed. This way you willna be accused of helping me escape. And things will be as they should be."

"I'll do no such thing," Alex replied, a little harsher than he intended. "If I take you back, they'll put you in irons until Imbolc, then toss you in the well to appease the old hag. That is not going to happen while I have the power to stop it."

"But you dinna understand, Alex. I've always known the day would come when I was called upon to offer my life for the benefit of the clan. I am ready to do that now."

"Well I'm not ready to let you go. I just found you, Ciara." Alex reached out to her, but she brushed his hand away.

"I should never have let you talk me into leaving the well."

"I'm glad I did." Alex said. "Call me daft, but now that I have found you, I want to spend the rest of my life with you. If you want to talk about fate and destiny, let's, because I believe you are my destiny." He thumped his fist against his chest.

"Perhaps you are mad," Ciara answered after a lengthy pause. She turned her back to him.

"Fine. But you are not going back to Burghead. At least not tonight." Getting nowhere, Alex dished out two bowls of porridge, slammed them on the table, and plunked himself down. "Sit and eat."

"I'm na hungry or thirsty." Ciara continued to stand. "You may be the son of Laird Innes, but you have no say in what I do. If I choose to go back, I will, and nothing is going to stop me." She crossed her arms over her chest and raised her chin in a show of defiance.

"Starving yourself will prove nothing." Alex shoved the stool beside him away from the table and gestured to it. "You're right, Ciara. I canna force you to do something you don't want to do. But I wish you'd eat something before it gets cold. Please." He scooped up another spoonful of oats and put it in his mouth. But he could not keep his eyes off Ciara. Hell, even when she was angry, she was beautiful. And he seemed to have a knack for antagonizing her.

Ciara huffed, then sat, but instead of eating, she folded her hands in her lap and stared at the bowl before her. "I want to go back, Alex." She picked up a spoon and swirled it in the porridge.

Seeing her in such turmoil caused his heart to ache. If only he could say something that would ease her mind and her conscience, convince her that her death was both not necessary, and would be a great loss. Not only to her family and clan, but to him as well. But it seemed the more he said, the worse he made things. If anything, he'd acted like an insensitive ass.

He slid his hand over hers and gave it a squeeze. "I know this is a ritual on which you've been raised, but as I told you before, I honestly believe the spring will come whether you forfeit your life or not. It's just basic science. Seasons change no matter what we do, or in this case, don't do."

A puzzled expression crossed Ciara's face. "What is science? You speak strangely and use words I have never heard before. Are they from an ancient tongue?"

Alex was surprised she hadn't asked sooner. His ancient Gaelic was rudimentary at best, and he frequently caught himself using words from the twenty-first century. Eventually, he'd have to tell her the truth, but this was not the right time, so he lied. "I traveled a lot when I was a boy…I mean a lad. Have you ever been anywhere but Burghead?"

"Nay. There was never a need."

"That would explain why I sound odd to you at times." Alex didn't see anything wrong with a little white lie if it eased her concerns. "I fostered for a time with Clan Forbes, then my father sent me to stay with a dear friend in the southern part of Scotland where I fostered with Clan Douglas."

"I suppose that would affect how one speaks," she replied. "But it doesna explain why you are so set against the ancient customs carried out by our people for centuries."

He shrugged. "I'm not being critical of ancient customs. It's just that I believe a man's life is governed by his own actions."

"Without traditions we have naught."

Alex slid two fingers beneath her chin and raised it until their eyes met. "Life is what you make it, Ciara."

"Is it? You say you govern your own life, but you are the son of a laird. Someday, you will be called upon to sit in your father's place and assume his role as chief. Whether you want to or na."

"We could argue this forever and never agree. But I don't understand how you knew you'd be chosen to be the one who must die." Nothing he had ever learned about the twelfth century could validate many of the things he'd heard and seen since his arrival, but he decided to listen, rather than challenging Ciara's story. She believed too deeply to be swayed.

"I am an oldest daughter and, as such, it is my destiny."

"I thought you were selected because you were caught trespassing at the well and took the sacred water for your ailing father. You are your clan's healer are you not?"

"Aye. And the water was also needed to purify the earth during the Imbolc festival," she said. "But your father locked me away because he feared I might use the water to thwart the winter hag." She lowered he gaze and wrung her hands. "But he was wrong. I would have offered myself on Imbolc, as is my destiny."

"I still don't understand how you came to be the chosen maiden. Alex scrubbed his hand across his chin. This simply made no sense to him. He was an archeologist and he was more familiar with the history of Scotland than many people who lived here. Human sacrifices simply were not a part of this culture. And even if they were, why did it have to be Ciara? "

"Why would you ask me such a thing?" She looked up at him, frowning. "Surely you know the legend."

"Of course I do," he replied. Though he only knew what Blair had told him. None of this had ever been recorded in historical documentation.

"Then you know that the winter hag was able to drink from the sacred well on Imbolc and have a season of youth as long as the talisman remained in the water. And you are also aware that changed when the gem disappeared twenty-one years ago."

He felt like he'd been gut-kicked. Could the amulet he had hidden in his chamber be the sacred talisman she spoke of? Was this why he was sent back in time, to return the gem to the well and set things to right? To save Ciara's life? "Damn." he cursed beneath his breath, wishing he hadn't left it behind. He couldn't be certain if it was the sacred stone, but once he knew she was safe, he'd have to go back for it. "It disappeared so long ago, yet the hag has waited until now to demand another maiden?"

"There was enough water stored to appease her while we searched for the talisman, but it was never found. Now the only way for her to gain the youth she desires is to work her magic and she needs young woman for that. An oldest daughter or a youngest daughter, a virgin, who has lived no less than eighteen and no more than twenty-one summers, a lass who offers herself willingly. The young woman must be sacrificed in the sacred well just after midnight on Imbolc allowing the Cailleach to steal her youth. One full year for each year of the girl's life."

"It makes no sense why anyone would ever agree to such a thing."

"The very reason Cailleach leveled her threat. If she doesna get what she wants, she will keep the land in her icy grip, preventing spring from coming and locking us in eternal winter."

"But that still doesn't explain why you? Why now?"

"The store of water is gone, I'm an oldest daughter, and I've seen twenty-one summers, m'lord. It is my duty, nay, my destiny, to do this for the good of the clan," she answered.

"Is that why you never married?"

She nodded. "When the talisman disappeared and the hag threatened to resume the sacrifices, a search was made throughout the land for maidens who would be the right age when the time came. Over the years some of the chosen died. Other clans, including your own, made certain their women failed to remain pure. Soon, only a few suitable lasses remained." She cocked her head and looked at Alex. "But you already know how the custom works. Why do you ask me to explain what has always been done."

He needed to bluff. "I may know about the ritual, but I know nothing about you or your family. You mentioned your younger sister. Do you have any others?" he asked, hoping not only to learn more about her, but to change the subject if possible.

"I am one of nine. Three lassies and six lads."

"And you're the oldest?"

"Nay. I was the fifth bairn born. There were three brothers who came before me and a sister." Ciara bowed her head and closed her eyes for a moment, a tear tracked her cheek. "Ila died when she was but eight summers. She caught the fever and there was nothing anyone could do to save her. The village seer said it was because she wasna worthy and pure of heart. She went as far as to say that Ila died so I could take her place." She shook her head and swiped the back of her hand across her face. "I dinna believe my sister was a bad person. She was my dearest friend and I still miss her."

"I'm sorry for your loss." Alex caressed the back of her hand. He'd never had any brothers or sisters, but if he did, he was sure it would hurt like hell to lose one.

"When Ila died, I became the oldest daughter and it was my duty to take her place." Ciara rose and stood before the hearth, staring into the flames. "If I dinna go back, my sister, Mairi will be forced to give up her life. She is the youngest daughter, has lived eighteen summers, and she too is pure of heart and soul. I couldna bear knowing I was the cause of her death. I wish you understood."

"I do understand the reason you think you need to go back." Alex approached Ciara from behind and slid his arms around her waist, resting his chin atop her head. "You couldn't bear to see Mairi die, knowing you might have stopped it, any more than I could stand seeing you perish, knowing I could have prevented it from happening." He blew out a heavy sigh. "You're not responsible for Mairi's fate or happiness, only for your own."

"That is what my mam told me. She said, in spite of your father's orders, other parents ensured their daughters wouldna be eligible. She wanted to hide us both away, but my father refused to hear of it. He actually believed it was an honor to be chosen. Despite how much our mother begged, he refused to listen, saying it would bring disgrace upon our family. That is another reason why I must go back." Ciara released a shuddered breath and relaxed against his chest as if she belonged in his arms.

"Your mother is wise. Nothing and no one should require her to make such a sacrifice. You should listen to her and allow me to see you safely hidden." Alex inhaled deeply, the delicate scent of lavender and heather filling his nostrils. His heart quickened and his groin stirred. All he could think about was scooping her up in his arms and carrying her to the bed. Were they to make love, she'd no longer be a virgin and Cailleach would have to choose another. But first he had to convince her to stay.

Alex gently turned Ciara in his arms and gazed down at her. "Come away with me, Ciara. Let me hide you, then I'll go back for Mairi as I promised I would. She can live with us until she meets a man, marries and has many babes. She'll die an old woman surrounded by her grandchildren. As will you."

"I always wanted bairns, but never harbored hopes of having any. Nor did I think about the prospects of growing old."

"Believe, sweetheart, it can all be yours someday if that's what you want." He gazed into emerald eyes a man could lose himself in and trailed his knuckle along her cheek. "Was there ever a man you loved and thought you might like to marry?"

She shook her head. "I was na allowed to associate with the men of my village. My father forbade it. I had never been kissed until today in the cave." She touched her lips and blushed. My father told me kissing would lead to temptation and sin."

"Then let me tempt you, lass." He lowered his head and lightly brushed his lips across her mouth. Pleased when she didn't pull away, he repeated the act a little more zealously, this time tickling the seam of her lips with his tongue.

Ciara stiffened and placed her palms on his chest. "This is wrong. We must stop."

"When a man and woman share a kiss, it's the most natural thing in the world. But if you want me to stop, I will." Saying those words gutted him, but he'd abide by her wishes, no matter what they were. He eased his hold on her, giving her some space and a chance to decide. But when she furled her finger in the fabric of his tunic and tugged him closer, he knew they'd only just begun.

Chapter Eight

Alex awakened and glanced down at Ciara. Tucked snuggly at his side, she slept like she didn't have a care in the world. He swept a lock of hair from her brow and replaced it with his lips. While Ciara was so exhausted she nodded off before he had a chance to make love to her, Alex was content knowing there was a chance they had a future together.

He closed his eyes and drew in a slow deep breath. "I must be a saint or out of my ever-loving mind," he mumbled, remembering the events of last evening and how it had taken every ounce of self-control he could muster not to ravage her body and make her his own. After an intense interlude of kissing and petting, he'd convinced her to join him on the bed. He promised if she agreed, he be a gentleman and not make inappropriate advances unless it was what she wanted. Not an easy task, given the way his body reacted to her presence.

Alex smiled. Perhaps when she awakened, they could pick up where they left off. "A man can hope," he chuckled.

The door to the croft opened, hitting the wall behind it with a crash.

"What the hell!" Alex shot up in bed, his eyes focused on the intruder. "Cailleach," he gasped. The old hag was the last person he wanted to see.

"I warned you na to interfere in things that you canna possibly understand," Cailleach hissed. "I told you to go back where you belong. Now you must pay the price."

Ciara sat up, hugging the pelt beneath her chin. "You two know each other?"

"We've met," Alex replied, his gaze focused on the hag.

"And you dinna see fit to tell me?" Ciara climbed off the bed, taking the pelt with her, and backed away. "I trusted you, but you obviously deceived me. You promised to protect me from Cailleach, not lead me into her grasp, like a lamb to slaughter. I was even beginning to think that you truly cared for me."

"I do care about you and at no time meant to deceive you. Please hear me out." He sprang from the bed and moved in her direction. "I didn't say anything about meeting Cailleach because I hoped never to cross paths with her again," Alex explained. "If I'd known she'd show up here, I would never have stopped."

"This is my croft. Where else would I be?" Cailleach asked. "You took something that belongs to me and I want it back."

"Ciara does not belong to you and never will," Alex countered. He held his hand out in Ciara's direction, but she backed away. If he had it all to do again, he'd have told her about his encounter with Cailleach. Now, he had to convince her.

"I should have known better than to trust the son of my enemy. You played me for a fool, Alex, and I let my people down." Tears welling in her eyes, Ciara lowered her gaze. "I'm so ashamed."

"You can trust me. And you've done nothing wrong, Ciara. I've never met a woman so brave and selfless in my entire life." Alex advanced, but she continued to back away until her spine rested against the wall and she could go no farther.

Cailleach inched closer, scowled, and pointed a boney finger at Alex. "Lies. He isna who he claims to be and was duly warned to go back from whence he came."

"I *am* Alex Innes. You mustn't listen to her, Ciara. She's only trying to confuse you," Alex said. "Cailleach is the one who can't be trusted. She means to kill you for her own selfish pleasure, and would say anything to get you to believe her and not me."

"He may bear the name Alex Innes, but isna who he claims to be," the hag snapped. "He is na from this time or place."

"What does she mean?" Ciara inclined her head, pinning Alex with her stare.

"I can explain," he said, unable to control the hint of desperation in his voice.

"And as for selfish pleasure," Cailleach cut in. "He lured you into this bed and meant to defile you, to take your maidenhead so you'd no longer be a worthy offering. He cared na if he disgraced you before your clan or forced your sister to take your place. He told me he had a task to complete before he could return to his own realm. Perhaps tricking you was part of his plan all along."

"Maybe I was sent to save Ciara, not betray her." He suddenly realized why he was here. He *had* been sent to save her, he was certain of it."

"If what she says is true, and you are na who you claim to be, then who are you?" Ciara asked. "I sensed something different in the way you spoke and behaved from the moment we met. But you assured me it was because you'd traveled a great deal and fostered in the south of Scotland for several years when you were a lad."

"Is that what he told you?" Cailleach cackled. "I gave you more credit than that, Alex. Actually, I thought you might prove a worthy match for me, and a wee bit of a challenge. I am so tired of the subservient, simpering fools who serve me for a season then turn tail as I age again." She held out her hand to Ciara. "Come, Imbolc is upon us and we have a ritual to perform at the sacred well."

While the hag was momentarily focused on Ciara, Alex grabbed his sword from the pile of garments on the floor and stepped between them, shielding Ciara with his body. "She's not going anywhere with you. Not while I still have a breath in my body." He quickly glanced over his shoulder at Ciara.

"Don't listen to her. I can explain everything if given the chance."

"Come now. You dinna think I can be so easily subdued. If that were so, I'd have been defeated centuries ago." The hag focused on the weapon in Alex's hand and mumbled an incantation in an ancient Gaelic tongue. One he'd never learned.

The blade began to glow, changing color from silver to crimson red, unbearable heat emanating along its length, and swiftly moving to the hilt. Unable to hold on to weapon any longer, Alex dropped it. "These are but magic tricks, meant to baffle and confuse," he said. "But I'll not be easily thwarted by your witchcraft. Ciara is not going with you."

"I am far more skilled than any witch and grow tired of this game." Cailleach raised her hands in the air, sparks shooting from her fingertips and striking Alex in the chest. "I'll no longer tolerate your interference in what is an ancient tradition. Things you know naught about and canna possibly understand."

A sudden wave of excruciating pain caused Alex to crumple to his knees in agony. Gasping for air, he clutched at his chest. If he didn't know better, he'd swear he was having a heart attack. But he'd not surrender. He gritted his teeth and glared up at Cailleach. "Is that the best you can do?"

"Stop, you're killing him." Ciara rushed to Alex and knelt at his side. "Dinna try to fight her. She possesses powers no mortal man can challenge." Tears running down her cheeks, she peered up at the hag. "Do with me as you will, but spare Alex."

"She is wiser than I thought," Cailleach said. "If I were you, I'd listen to the lass. Her willingness to forgive your deception and offer her life for yours proves she is a suitable choice for the Imbolc Ceremony." She lowered her arm.

As the pain subsided, Alex clasped Ciara's forearm. "It doesn't matter what she spell she casts, don't go with her,

Ciara. Promise me."

Ciara wrenched free of his grasp and rose. "I'm afraid I canna let her kill you, Alex. She will do with me as she pleases, regardless of whether you live or die. Just like night will always turn to day. You taught me that. I was a fool for coming with you in the first place." She lowered her gaze. "I am the chosen one, the one she wants, and there is no point in you giving up your life for naught."

"It doesn't have to be that way, Ciara. Alone neither of us may be her match, but together, I believe we can defeat her." Alex tried to stand, but his legs gave way and he slumped to the ground. In addition to inflicting pain, the hag had drained the strength from his body.

"You defied your father and I have disgraced myself and my clan. I can never go home and neither can you," Ciara said. "I have no choice but to do as she commands. It is destined, and so it must be done."

"No. I'll not accept your defeat or mine. There must be a way I can take you back with me."

"Back to where?"

The words slipped out before Alex could stop them. It was too late to rescind them, and judging by the shocked expression on Ciara's face, he had to continue.

"I did not come to Scotland to interfere with the ancient customs of my ancestors or to disturb the past. I came to study them," Alex said. But it was clear he was making things worse not better, when Ciara cupped her hand over her mouth and stared at him as if in shock. "I also came to replace an amulet to its rightful resting place."

"An amulet? Do you mean the Talisman of Light?"

"It's just a ruby pendant."

Cailleach waved her hand over Alex's face, staring at him as if viewing the contents of his thoughts. "You *do* have the Druid talisman? I can see it." She held out her hand. "Give it to me. *Now*. It is mine."

"I don't have it with me. But I can get it," Alex said. Perhaps he had a bargaining chip after all. "You obviously seem interested, but how do I know it was meant for you?"

"It is mine. It was stolen from my well and I demand you give it to me at once," Cailleach reiterated harshly.

"Alex, if you have the Talisman of Light, and return it to the well, Cailleach will be able to drink the water to gain her season of youth instead of taking a life."

"Nay. It belongs to me and I will choose whether it is returned to the well or not. Cailleach hissed.

"But the amulet was stolen and we've searched for it for years," Ciara blurted, then addressed Alex. "Did you steal the talisman from the well?"

"Of course not. I wasn't even born yet. *Not until centuries later.*" The last part of his statement he mumbled under his breath. "It was unearthed by a peer of my father's and taken from Scotland. I don't know where he found it, but my dad wanted me to return it."

Scotland was a country deep rooted in superstition and rituals. So it was possible that not everything in history was recorded accurately or even recorded at all. Was the story of the amulet one of those legends that slipped through the cracks? If so, it would explain a lot, including why he'd never heard of it until now and why things were not as they were historically documented. He'd often heard that if past is changed, the future is also affected. Perhaps the removal of the talisman by his father's colleague changed the course of history.

Ciara glared at him. "You said the talisman was taken from Scotland and your father bid you return it. That means Laird Innes has known all along where it was and lied to his people. He'd have seen me sacrificed in order to keep his secret," Ciara blurted. "That also means you lied to me and let me go on about the legend and my family. You've had it all along and could have returned it and ended all of this, but—"

"I know this will all seem hard to grasp, but I beg you to listen to what I have to say before passing judgment," Alex pleaded. "I didn't steal the amulet and neither did Laird Innes. But I was asked to return it. I fully intended to do that as soon as I found out where it belonged. But the plane crashed and I ended up here in the twelfth century. Then I met you, Ciara, and it was like we'd known each other forever. When I found out you were to be offered to the hag, I couldn't stand by and watch you die because of archaic superstition. I didn't know about the power of the amulet until you told me legend last night. Once I made sure you were safe, I planned retrieve it and give it Cailleach in exchange for your life. You must believe me."

"I told you he was not who he pretends to be," Cailleach said, grinning.

"You've deceived me and mock our beliefs, yet want me to trust you?" Ciara frowned and backed away. "Are you telling me that everything Cailleach has been saying is true? Who are you really, and where are you from?"

"That is exactly what he is confessing," Cailleach said before Alex could answer. "Now you know the truth, I order you to come with me. The hour grows late. And while you may never be able to return to your family without shame, there is but a few hours left to complete the ritual and put an end to winter."

The strength slowly returning to his legs, Alex rose. He had to make Ciara understand and confront Cailleach on her own level, face-to-face. "Don't listen to her, Ciara. If the legend is true, the amulet was offered in exchange for the life of the maiden, not in addition to it." He stared at the hag. "If I get you the gem, will you spare Ciara's life?"

"Enough! I will have both." Cailleach raised her hands again, this time the gesture was accompanied by a blinding flash of light.

Pain lanced through his head, ricocheting around his skull. Alex grabbed his forehead and collapsed to the ground, darkness enveloping him.

~ * ~

Alex moaned, his arm thrown across his forehead, shielding his eyes from the rays of sunlight sneaking past the shutters. He wasn't sure which hurt more, his head or his chest. "This trip to Scotland has taken a hell of a toll on my body. If I ever manage to find the way back to my own time period, I'm booking a long vacation to somewhere hot and exotic," he mumbled aloud, then rolled to his side.

"My time period," he muttered. "Shit. Ciara." Alex used the side of the bed to haul himself to an upright position, but momentarily lost his balance. His head spinning, he sat on the edge of the mattress, waiting for the brain fog to clear. When he could finally see straight, he scanned the room, looking for Ciara and the hag. But he was very much alone. Not that he was surprised.

Panic pierced his gut as he picked up his tunic and tugged it over his head. He fastened the sword at his side and donned his boots. There was no telling how long he'd been passed out on the floor, but he guessed it had been a while. The hag would make sure she had long enough to abscond with Ciara and get to the well.

Time being of the essence, Alex hurried across the room and threw open the door, a blast of cold air stealing his breath. The storm was over and the sun was shining, but the celestial orb also hung low in the sky.

It was much later in the day than Alex had hoped. If he was to make his way back to the castle, retrieve the amulet, and save Ciara before the stroke of midnight he'd have to make haste. Getting into the keep and out again unnoticed was not going to be easy, if it was even possible. But he had to try. Ciara's life depended on it. If he failed, she would perish. Something he was not prepare to consider.

Alex sprinted off, running as fast as his legs would carry him and the drifts of snow would allow. As he neared the castle, he slowed his pace. Certain that after he'd escaped with Ciara, Laird Innes would have everyone looking for them, he needed to plan his moves carefully if he hoped to pull this off.

After scanning the parapets for sentries and seeing no one, Alex dashed for the postern gate. He entered the bailey, then crouched in some bushes, hoping to remain out of sight. Since there was no telling when the guards might pass by again, he waited and watched.

Minutes seemed like hours, but he could not be too careful. If found and turned over the laird, his quest to save Ciara would be over. After making another quick search of the grounds and praying it was safe to do so, Alex bolted for the storage room door at the rear of the keep.

While he had not been at the castle long enough to know his way around, Alex had examined sketches and speculative blueprints of how it was constructed when he had visited the University archives. Having a personal interest in the Clan Innes history and anything else he could get his hands on, he'd studied the drawings at great length before leaving on his trip, and was glad he had. This knowledge would prove most useful.

If he recalled correctly, a series of tunnels and hidden passageways were built into the structure, a means of escape for the laird and his family in the event of an attack. Now, if he could just locate the secret door leading into and out of the kitchen storage room, he'd be happy.

He scratched his head and studied each wall in turn, pausing when he spotted what he was searching for. Unlike the rest of the irregular shaped fieldstones used to fashion the foundation, he noticed a series of square cut stones, arranged in the shape of a cross, and partially hidden from view by a stack of wine barrels. If the plans for the keep were accurate, Alex was certain if he moved the barrels, he'd find a small wooden door located near the floor—large enough for a man to crawl through.

Confident he'd located the entrance to the passageway, he started across the room, but ducked behind a crock of pickled turnips when he heard someone coming. Unfortunately, as he dove for cover his foot caught a broom and sent it crashing to the floor.

The servant raised his torch. "Is someone in here?" he called out, then moved in Alex's direction.

Afraid he'd be seen, Alex fingered the hilt of his sword, prepared to pounce if necessary. He didn't want to harm the man, or anyone, as far as that went, but nothing short of death would stand in the way of rescuing Ciara. Holding his breath, he watched as the servant got closer. Alex might have been found had not a rat, the size of an alley cat, scurried over the toe of his boot, then crossed the servant's path.

"Damned rodents." The servant picked up the broom and pummeled the animal until it lay lifeless on the floor. "That'll teach you," he grumbled. Obviously satisfied he'd caught the intruder, the man kicked it aside, grabbed a side of mutton from a hook hanging from the ceiling, and left the storeroom.

Alex rocked back on his heels, releasing the breath he'd been holding. He waited until he was certain the man did not return and prayed no one else came along to hinder his mission. Confident the coast was clear, he crawled on hands and knees to the wine barrels and quickly rolled two of the oak containers away from the wall.

Chapter Nine

Relieved to find the entrance to the secret passageway, Alex used the dirk he'd stashed in his boot to pry open the wooden door and entered the dark damp space. Spider webs brushed his face and shivers ran down his spine. He was never fond of arachnids, but knowing the place was likely infested with rats and other disgusting vermin was even worse. The smell of mold, dust, and rodent dropping assaulted his nostrils, but he kept crawling until he saw a bit of light filtering through some cracks in the chinking a few feet ahead of him.

When he reached the lit area, he noticed the ceiling of the tunnel was high enough for him to stand. Feeling his way along the stone wall, he headed for another spot a little farther away, one that he assumed was a doorway, given the size of the square rim of light surrounding it. As he got closer, he bumped his head on the roof of the tunnel, the height of which apparently decreased as he neared the exit. Dropping to his knees again, he crawled the rest of the way.

Alex reached the end of the passageway and paused to listen for the sound of voices. He wasn't certain, but if memory served him, this tunnel came out near the stairs leading to the above floor. He rested on his heels, hoping it was safe to leave, when he noticed a set of stone steps to his right. Upon further investigation, he deduced they lead to the above floor and likely came out in or near the laird's chamber.

Alex took the stairs two at a time, then followed a short passageway that ended with another door. After a quick survey of his surroundings, he concluded this was the only way out and pushed until the small wooden slab moved an inch—enough for him to see it was blocked by a wooden chest, and as he suspected, it opened into the laird's chamber.

Given the time of day, Alex figured his father would be in the great hall, preparing for the evening meal. He mumbled a prayer that he was right, and using his shoulder, leaned into the door with all the strength he could muster.

The barrier gave way, and Alex toppled out, landing on his back and staring at the ceiling. After getting his bearings, he leapt to his feet and padded to the door. Opening it a crack, he peered into the hallway. Once the coast was clear, he left his father's room, entered his own chamber, and headed straight for the bed in search of the talisman.

"What in damnation are you doing here?"

Alex stiffened and spun around to face his cousin Blair. "I wish you would stop sneaking up from behind and scaring the shit out of me."

"I wish you would stop taking chances and putting your life in danger," Blair countered. "You dinna answer my question. What the hell are you doing here and where is the lass? I went to great lengths to cover for you, but I think your da is suspicious. It was foolish of you to return right now."

"I don't have time to explain everything," Alex said as he lifted the mattress and snatched up his leather jacket. He searched the breast pocket, retrieving the stone. "Cailleach has Ciara and I had to come back for this." He loosened the drawstring and tipped the sack, the gem tumbling onto his palm. "It's her only hope. I just pray I can get there before it's too late."

"Make time to explain," Blair snapped. "And what have you got there?" He peered over Alex's shoulder at the gem in his hand. "Shite, man, that is the missing Talisman of Light. Where did you get it?"

"I told you I don't have time to explain," Alex repeated. He stared at the talisman. If removing it from Scotland had such a dramatic influence on history, would turning the gem over to Cailleach and rescuing Ciara set things to right or make things worse? He returned the gem to the pouch, and after fastening it to his sash, tucked it into the waist of his trews for safekeeping "Now that I've gotten what I came for, I can go back to the well and hopefully save Ciara."

Alex spun around, fully intending to leave the same way he entered, but ran smack into his father and the two guards who'd been standing sentry at the well.

"Not so fast," the laird growled. "You are na going anywhere. Especially na to the well to save the Dunmore lass."

"Is she there? Have you seen her?" Alex asked. "The hag is going to kill her if I don't help her."

"What interest do you have in this woman? Why does it matter if she lives or dies?" the laird asked. "This must be done and you have no right to question it, or to interfere. Who do you think you are?"

Damn it, Alex knew that wasn't right. Human sacrifice in the old world had not survived into the twelfth century. He had to try to stop this. "I am nobody, my laird. But she's done naught to deserve this. Even the Druids sought to prevent the ritual by making a ruby talisman to appease the hag in her quest for youth and save a lass's life." Alex bit his lower lip to keep from saying any more. If he'd learned anything since his arrival in the twelfth century, challenging the laird's authority or beliefs would not help his cause. But there had to be a way to reason with him, to get the laird to at least consider the reason for his actions.

"Nay," the laird growled. "I've had enough of your interference. I will not risk eternal winter. This must be done."

It wasn't done. It can't be done, was on the tip of Alex's tongue, but he couldn't say it. "The talisman was stolen," Alex replied. He considered showing the gem to his father, but if his plan failed and the amulet was confiscated, it might not get to the well in time to save Ciara. "I wish I could make you understand."

"Silence." The laird raised his hand in the air. "I understand fully what you are saying. But the hag demands payment, and the ritual must take place. That is why I am ordering my men to throw you in the dungeon until after Imbolc has passed," his father said. "Hopefully, you will have time to think about what you've done and how close you came to sentencing the people of this clan to eternal winter."

"You're a smart and sensible man, Father. Perhaps the most cunning and clever laird I know." Alex didn't think some flattery to boost his father's ego would hurt. "And I mean no disrespect to your or your beliefs by questioning your judgment. But isn't it possible that spring will still come anyway, regardless if the lass is sacrificed or not?"

"Watch it, cousin," Blair whispered. "You will only make things worse if you challenge your da's beliefs again."

"I'm not contradicting what he believes, just offering him some other options to consider," Alex said through clenched teeth. "There's nothing wrong with a laird who is open to new ideas."

Laird Innes glowered at Blair. "And what about you, nephew? Did you have anything to do with my son's foolish attempt to save the lass? Fergus and Donald claimed they were attacked by at least two men, perhaps more."

"That's a lie to save face." Since he was telling the truth, Alex had no problem looking the laird directly in the eye. It did only take one man to get the jump on them. Blair. "I acted alone. My cousin had no knowledge of my actions. As far as he knew, I was going hunting and nothing more."

The laird balled his fists and took a menacing step forward. "Lucky for him, or you would both wind up in irons. There is no good excuse for defying my orders. For that reason, son or na, you will be taken to the dungeon." He glanced at Fergus and motioned with a sweep of his hand.

"Take him now, see that he doesn't escape. He is to have no visitors. And that includes my nephew. Do I make myself clear?"

Fergus offered a curt nod. "Aye, m'lord." Your orders will be followed to the letter."

"See that they are this time," the laird growled. "While it pains me to do this, son, it is for your own good and that of the clan. If you are to be chief someday, I canna have you questioning me or going behind my back." He turned on his heel and left the chamber.

While Donald stood watch, Fergus relieved Alex of his sword. Fortunately he did not check his boot, nor did he notice the pouch containing the amulet. Not that it would do Alex any good. If locked in the dungeon, there was no way he could rescue Ciara. Fergus grabbed Alex by the upper arm. "Let's go, and dinna try anything. You'll na get the better of us twice. If you were na the laird's son, I'd beat you senseless first, then haul your sorry arse to the dungeon." He glared at Blair. "Best you be on your way. I'm na convinced Lord Alex acted on his own."

"Unhand me, you buffoon." Alex twisted free of Fergus's grasp. "If you were not following my father's instructions and I was still armed, I'd like to see you try to best me. Also keep in mind that what my da said is true. I'll someday be laird and you will find yourself cleaning garderobes for the rest of your sorry life if you don't learn to counsel your tongue."

Blair chuckled. "Well put, cousin."

Alex had to admit, the longer he kept the ruse going and let everyone think he was the laird's real son, the more natural it felt. But that didn't change the fact that he was destined for the dungeon and he was currently in no position to do anything about it. Ciara came to mind again. He had to figure out a way to escape and rescue her. If he could somehow convince Blair to go in his stead and offer

Cailleach the talisman, there might still be hope. But given his father's ban on visitors, that was not going to happen. Besides, Cailleach seemed to want both Ciara and the talisman and Alex hadn't had time to explain that.

"Move. The dungeons await," Fergus couldn't conceal a sly grin as he gave Alex a shove. Clearly, he took great pleasure in seeing Alex punished.

"Best you do as he says, cousin," Blair said and winked when Fergus and Donald were not looking. "I'll see you after." He faced the guards. "See that he gets there in one piece and unharmed, or you will have me to answer to." He patted the hilt of his sword and trotted down the hall ahead of them.

~ * ~

Alex sat on the floor of the dungeon for what seemed like hours, staring up at the only window in the hellhole. Daylight was all but gone and evening was upon them. He guessed Ciara had only a couple of hours before midnight, if that, and her life would be ended. A lump formed in his throat and raw emotion knotted his gut, his chest so tight he could hardly draw a breath.

He'd never been lucky in the romance department, despite his mother's undying efforts to set him up with every eligible, single young lady under the age of thirty at the country club she and his father belonged to. She wanted grandchildren in the worst way, but he was not about to marry a woman to satisfy his mother's whims. Nor had anyone ever sparked enough interest to tempt him to stray from his career or goals, until now.

At thirty-one, he'd certainly dated, but he had been too busy following in his father's footsteps, trying to become a world famous archeologist, so finding a wife took a back seat. He'd always thought he had plenty of time to find a woman and settle down. Perhaps get a house in the burbs and raise a couple of kids. But after meeting Ciara, he doubted he'd ever be satisfied again. Not to mention he seemed to be stuck in the twelfth century.

By now, his mother thought him dead, all hopes of having grandbabies to carry on the family name, dashed. He wondered how she was coping with the news of his death and prayed she was okay. But there was no way of knowing what was going on in the future. Perhaps by changing the past, he'd changed the future as well. For all he knew, maybe his parents had not met and he was never born. He once read somewhere that if you alter the past, the future is profoundly effected as well.

"Are you going to just sit there twiddling your thumbs and feeling sorry for yourself, or are you ready to get out of these gracious accommodations?" Blair laughed.

Alex sprang to his feet. "What are you doing here? How did you get past Laurel and Hardy, or need I ask?" The words comparing the guards to a twentieth century comedy team slipped out before he could stop them.

"While I again find your odd choice of words baffling, I took care of the guards if that is what you are asking." He dangled the ring of keys that unlocked the cell door. "Say please and I will let you out."

"Open the door, damn it. There is no time to jest." Alex grabbed onto the bars and rattled the door. "Ciara needs me, and there can't be much time left before midnight."

Blair jammed the key into the lock and gave it a twist, the door swinging open. "There is only about half an hour before midnight, so we will have to make haste."

"If you were going to risk your neck to free me, why did you wait so long?" Alex asked, a little more harshly than he intended. He didn't mean to sound ungrateful, but Blair had left things to the last minute, leaving him very little time to help Ciara.

"I wanted to wait until most of the castle was asleep and

the guards would be groggy," Blair replied with a grin. "I made sure of it by adding a wee bit of belladonna to a couple of mugs of ale. I then sent Maggie, the kitchen wench, to offer the guards a drink. Of course they couldna refuse either the ale or the lass." He wiggled a brow. "They are both out cold and we are free to pass."

"Then best we go while we can." Alex brushed by Blair, almost knocking his cousin off his feet. He rushed down the corridor, past the two guards, and sprinted up the stairs, with Blair on his heels.

When they reached the main corridor of the castle, Blair placed his hand on Alex's shoulder, forcing him to pause. "Hold. Let me check to see the coast is clear. The last thing we need is someone waking your da and telling him you have escaped. Once we've rescued the lass and you are away, I will return to my chamber and climb into bed. That way when the guards wake up and sound the alarm, I will be fast asleep in my room. Or so they'll think."

Blair opened the door and peered into the hallway. "There is no one around. Let's go." He darted down the hall and out of castle.

Alex followed, but when they reached the bailey he stopped.

Blair came to an abrupt halt and whipped around to face Alex. "Come on, there is na time to dally. It takes at least ten minutes to reach the well."

"We are not going anywhere. I need to do this alone, Blair. I must face Cailleach on her turf and do it on my own if I have any hope of saving Ciara."

"I've come this far and am na going to turn back now. Go without me if you wish, but I will follow," Blair snapped. "So we can either go together and stop wasting time or continue to argue and miss the chance to stop the hag from throwing Ciara in the well. The choice is yours."

"You're a stubborn, hardheaded, fool," Alex said.

"Aye. And where would you be right now without me?" Blair countered.

"I have to admit you have a point." Alex raked his fingers through his hair. "Without your help, I would never have been able to rescue Ciara from the well the other day, and would be sitting in the dungeon as we speak."

"Then let's be away, cousin."

"You can come, Blair. But only under one condition. When we reach the well, I need you to wait outside. Do you agree not to interfere?"

Blair nodded. "Aye, you have my word on it."

"Fine. Let's go." Alex took off running. He intended to offer the talisman in exchange for Ciara's life, but if the hag refused or he sensed for one minute that she intended to double cross him, he planned to catch her off guard, tackle her about the waist, and hurl them both into the well. He'd not relinquish his hold until Cailleach stopped struggling and sank like a stone. And while he might drown in the process, Ciara would live, he'd honor the promise made to his father, and the amulet would be where the Druids intended.

Chapter Ten

Ciara stood with her back pressed against the wall of the cave, watching Cailleach pace in front of the entranceway, mumbling in Gaelic. She'd given up all hope of being rescued and just wanted to get the inevitable over and done. "If you mean to kill me, why na do it now and get it over with."

The hag paused and glared at Ciara. "I fully intend to toss you into the well and allow the demons of the netherworld to drag you down. But it must be done after midnight on the second day of February and not before, or the magic willna work."

"I'll be dead and you will be honor bound to release the land from winter. What difference does it make when you do the deed?"

"If I were to do it now, I'd not be granted the favor of your beauty, youth, and vitality for the next twenty-one years," the hag snapped. "I accepted the talisman in exchange for a virgin eons ago and it teased me with brief glimpses of youth."

"And if Alex gives it back to you, you will have that again."

"That's not enough," Cailleach spat. "I want the perpetual youth I'll gain from your sacrifice and that of those who follow you. What I failed to understand when I agreed to the exchange was that after I'd drunk from the well once, I must continue to do it forever unless I have a suitable sacrifice. But should the time come when a worthy virgin is not available, the talisman will continue to give me what I need."

"What if Alex doesna give you back to you?"

"He will give it back. A fool in love makes many

mistakes."

"And if he refuses, what happens if there are no suitable sacrifices after me?"

Her smirk of satisfaction turned to a scowl. "If I have neither a virgin nor the talisman, it isn't only that I won't gain the youth I desire, I will lose my immortality altogether. That is why the amulet was so important. I was the one who hid it years ago when I desired the stronger magic, but it disappeared. Without its power or the Imbolc ritual sacrifice, I will wither up and die."

"You hid it? To ensure you'd be offered a virgin sacrifice to remain young? So if you have neither, you will cease to exist?" Her mind reeling, Ciara contemplated jumping into the well before the stroke of midnight. Taking her own life was certainly not appealing, but she'd be spending eternity at the bottom of the well anyway, so it didn't really matter. If her death meant Cailleach would perish too, so be it. She shuffled toward the lip of the sacred pool.

Cailleach raised her hand and pointed her finger at Ciara. "Dinna even think about hurling yourself into the well. Move any closer and you will live to regret it. Even if it is for just a few more minutes. Mark my words, lass, they will be the worst minutes imaginable." The hag left her spot by the entrance to the cave and moved to within inches of where Ciara stood and again pointed at the dark water.

Ciara continued to stare at her reflection in the pool. Perhaps the hag was lying to save her own pathetic hide. She, on the other hand, was going to die anyway, so had nothing to lose.

"Jump if you like," Cailleach hissed. "But as you leap, I will turn the water into granite, and you will shatter every bone in your body as you strike what was once a liquid surface. You will lie there writhing in agony until the time is right for me to take your soul. After which, I will turn the stone back into water again and watch you sink to your final resting place. There, you will wait until others join you. I never intend to appear as a hag again."

"If you damage my body, will that na make it worthless to you in the years to come?"

"It matters not what condition your physical form is in when you die. It is your soul and spirit that matter. I will emerge from this withered shell as you stand before me now. Every bit as lovely and strong."

Ciara backed away from the edge. Her time almost up, she dropped to her knees and began to pray. "Grant me the strength to die well and do my clan proud. If I have but one wish, it would be to see Alex one more time, to say goodbye and apologize for doubting his honor. But I know that isna possible."

"You are wasting your prayers and your breath," the hag spat. "You will never see Alex Innes again, nor will he save you from your destiny. Why, as we speak he is being held in his father's dungeon, and there he will stay until after the Imbolc festival is completed."

Ciara clutched a hand to her throat. "Alex was imprisoned by his own father because he helped me?" Her heart clenched.

"He defied his father and disgraced his clan. He is where he should be," the hag replied smugly. Her evil grin broadened. "But I wouldna fash over it. I'm sure in time, he will be released. Perhaps I will pay him a visit once you are gone and I have taken your soul. He will not recognize my face, because it will be as it was when I was a young lass, but he will warm to your body I am sure. I will get the talisman back from him."

"Alex is na a fool. He would know you for the evil witch you are."

"You may be right, but mortal men are driven by carnal needs above all else. I would wager he will sate those needs with me regardless of his opinion. It has been a while since I was bedded by anyone as handsome and virile as Alex Innes. I actually find the idea quite appealing." She closed her eyes and wrapped her arms around her middle, moaning aloud. "I long to feel his caress, to have him enter me on the most intimate level and plant his seed. To—"

"I'm afraid Hell would have to freeze over and the moon to fall out of the sky for there to be any chance of that." Alex appeared at the entrance to the cave.

"Go back, Alex. Leave while you can," Ciara shouted.

"Do as the lass says and I will deal with you later, much later," Cailleach said and stroked her breasts. You will lie with me if I so desire."

"I'd rather be stretched on a rack and have rats chew off my fingers and toes than bed the likes of you."

"That could also be arranged," Cailleach snarled.

"I'm sure it could, but first-things-first." Alex unhooked the velvet pouch from his sash and held it in the air. "I have something you want more than Ciara. Let her go and we'll negotiate."

"Show me. How do I know that that sack contains the talisman?" Cailleach lunged forward with her hand outstretched. "Give me."

"I will when you let Ciara go and she is far from this place. Once the clock strikes midnight and it is February the second, I will return the talisman to the well and you can drink your fill of the water." He returned the pouch to his sash. "Refuse and I will do as you asked me to on the day I met you—return from whence I came. I'll take the talisman with me and it will be lost to you forever."

"You wouldna dare risk my wrath. Do you forget what I did to you in the croft?" Cailleach asked. "I can do it again. Only this time, I will show no mercy. Make no mistake, I will not only kill the lass, but will have the talisman as well."

"That isn't part of the deal," Alex said. "I overheard you

telling Ciara about the history behind the gem and how the Druids intended it to be used. If I heard you correctly, once you started using the magic of the talisman, you must continue using it or have a young willing virgin to sacrifice. I promise you the day will come when you will not receive such an offering. Without the talisman, you will die." Alex crossed his arms over his chest. "Or am I wrong in my assumption?"

Cailleach grabbed Ciara and dragged her to the water's edge. "The midnight hour is nearly upon us. Give me the talisman or I will throw her into the water and have my years of beauty and health regardless."

"You would settle for twenty-one years and risk your immortality?" Alex asked.

"Dinna trust her Alex. She will kill me no matter what you do and still take the talisman the first chance she gets," Ciara said. "Please leave. If you challenge her, she will kill you too and I canna bear to watch you to die on my account."

"I knew I'd find you here." Laird Innes stood at the entrance to the cave, Fergus and Donald entering after, with Blair in tow.

Cailleach raised her arms, a churning of frigid air swirling about her like a small cyclone. "I order you all to leave. The ritual must be completed or I will condemn you to eternal winter. You have chosen this lass and she has offered her life to me. I accept her as worthy and demand I be allowed to finish what I've started." She began to chant, the wind whipping around faster and picking up bits of stone and debris from the ground.

"More magic tricks?" Alex scoffed.

Laird Innes grabbed Alex by the upper arm. "Dinna anger her. She is right. This ritual must be completed. We must leave now and allow Cailleach to finish." The laird tried to drag Alex away, but he dug in his heels.

"I'm not going anywhere. Not without Ciara." Alex

yanked free of his father's grasp and glared back at him. "If you're afraid of this old woman, leave. But she doesn't scare me and I don't believe in her magic. We can end this. We can end her. I have the Tal—"

"Silence. I've had enough of this. I'm your father and your laird. Continue to defy me and I'll have no choice but to punish you more severely this time. You are going to leave this place whether you wish to or not," the laird informed him. "Refuse to walk out of here of your own accord and I'll have Fergus carry you out over his shoulder if need be. Either way, you are leaving."

"Not without Ciara." Alex moved deeper into the cave.

"We'll see about that." Fergus leapt forward, tackling Alex to the ground. "You heard your father. We are leaving this place now and you are na going to interfere with the sacred ritual."

The two men grappled on the ground, coming dangerously close to the edge of the well on more than one occasion. Despite being outweighed by at least three stone, Alex refused to surrender. He was fighting to remain with the woman he loved, and somehow found the strength to fight back. Using a few of the wrestling moves he'd learned in university didn't hurt either.

"I demand you stop this at once," the laird said.

"It matters naught, the time of the sacrifice is nigh, Cailleach announced. She grasped Ciara by the collar of her gown and hauled her to the edge of the well. "The hour of sacrifice has arrived. I offer this virgin to you, the god of—"

"Wait!" Alex found the strength to throw Fergus over his shoulder, then staggered to his feet. He opened the pouch, took out the talisman to prove he really had it. "Push her in and you'll never get this."

Fergus rose and lunged at Alex again. It was clear he had more than following his laird's order in mind. The man was obviously determined to make Alex pay for giving him so much grief.

Alex dodged his first attempt, but found himself with his back against the wall and nowhere to go. He glanced at the talisman clenched tightly in his fist and as Fergus advanced and knew what he had to do. Perhaps it was the magic of the talisman at work, but he was certain, if he tossed it to Ciara and the willing sacrifice possessed the talisman, the hag wouldn't be able to use either brand of magic.

The gem landed at her feet, but Ciara swiftly scooped it up and put it around her neck.

Cailleach glowered at the gem. "That belongs to me and I want it now." She reached for the talisman, but she couldn't seem to touch it.

"Don't give it to her, Ciara. No matter what happens. It will protect you from her." He turned his attention back to the fight at hand, knowing Fergus would not give up until one or both of them were dead, Alex gritted his teeth, lowered his stance and charged forward, encircling his opponent's waist.

Caught off guard and knocked off balance, Fergus stumbled backward, toppling into the well. But as he did, he grabbed Alex's tunic and pulled him in as well.

Fergus refused to let go, pulling Alex under over and over again until he could no longer fight.

"Alex," Ciara shouted.

His name was the last word he heard as the water closed over his head. His lungs robbed of air, he prayed not for his own life, but that the talisman worked as he believed it would. Cailleach would be unable to touch Ciara or the talisman and as the sun rose on Imbolc, the winter hag would die.

Chapter Eleven

Alex groaned as he tried to suck in a short shallow breath, a crushing pain lancing across his chest. If he didn't know better, he'd swear his entire body was on a medieval rack with some sadistic bugger tightening the crank. Even his hair hurt. Nausea tugged at his belly and the slightest movement caused his head to pound like a hammer set to anvil.

"Lord be praised, he's waking up." A woman's voice filtered through the heavy fog clouding his mind. She clasped his hand and held it to her breast. "Can you hear me, love?"

He heard the desperation in her voice, recognized the scent of her rosewater cologne, and forced himself to open his eyes. "Mom?" he muttered.

"Yes, son, it's me. Your mother."

"Where…where am I?"

"In Scotland, dear. You're in the hospital. The plane crashed and I—" She was unable to finish, her voice quivering as she spoke.

"I remember." He narrowed his gaze, straining to focus on her face. "What are you doing here?"

"Where else would I be?" his mother replied. "As soon as they called and told me you were alive, I caught the first flight over."

"Your mam hasna left your side since they brought you back from surgery." A tall, middle-aged nurse carrying a metal tray entered the room and set it on the bedside table. She removed a small bag from a protective wrapping, rolled it between her hands to mix the contents, and hung it on the IV pole—replacing one that had run dry. After she adjusted the drip rate and checked the monitors, she faced Alex's mother. "This is a miracle, to be sure. He's breathing on his own and his vitals have stabilized."

"Thank God." His mother gazed skyward and folded her hands in prayer. "I was so afraid I might lose him."

The nurse patted Mrs. Innes's shoulder and smiled. "It was touch and go for a while, but this sudden improvement in his condition is a welcome turn of events. Doctor Murray will be most pleased."

Alex glanced around the room. Judging by the overpowering scent of antiseptic, the large window with a view of a nursing station directly across the hallway, and the array of elaborate machinery surrounding his bed, it appeared he was in the hospital's intensive care unit.

"But none of this makes any sense." Alex brought a shaky hand to his brow. His throat was so dry, he'd give anything for a sip of water.

"Accidents seldom do." His mother stroked his cheek. "You've been through a lot, son. I'm sure it will all come back to you in a day or so."

"Your mam is right. Dinna try to talk. You need to conserve your strength," the nurse said. "The pain medicine in the IV bag should start working soon. Rest now."

"I don't want to rest," Alex replied sharply. "The events of the last few days are very clear in my mind and I didn't spend them in a hospital bed. Aside from a few bumps and bruises, I walked away from the crash and left the airport in the rental vehicle my secretary arranged."

"Alex, please. You don't have to do this now," his mother cautioned.

"I need to do this before the drugs muddle my mind." Alex drew in a gulp of air, then continued. "I thought I could make it to the dig site, but got stuck in a snow bank on my way. Fortunately, I found refuge in an old croft and that is where I spent the first night."

He sucked in another slow shallow breath and continued. "In the morning, I borrowed a horse and went on to

Burghead. That's where I spent the last couple of days. In a Medieval Scottish castle, living amongst people in the twelfth century." He stopped there when he noticed the look of horror and disbelief on his mother's face. He had to confess, the latter statements gave him pause for thought as well. The story sounded crazy to him, and he'd been there. The nurse and his mother were sure to think him mad.

"There, there, you must try to relax." The nurse rested her hand on Alex's shoulder as she offered him a sympathetic glance, and spoke to his mother. "Try na to worry, Mrs. Innes. It's na uncommon for a patient to be confused and disoriented after a severe trauma. They imagine all sorts of things, and are convinced they really happened. Try na to fash, your son will be more lucid after he's had time to recover."

"Even as a boy, he had a vivid imagination. I suppose an event like this can't help," his mother said.

"I imagined nothing." Alex found himself getting more agitated and frustrated by the minute. "And I wish you would stop talking about me like I'm not in the room. Other than a bump on the head and some sore ribs, I was not injured when the plane crashed. And I did spend the last few days in—"

"Calm down, Mr. Innes, or I will have to administer something stronger to relax you," the nurse said. "The plane crash happened over two weeks ago and you have gone nowhere except radiology and the operating theater."

"Please do as the nurse requests, Alex," his mother said. "Perhaps you were dreaming."

"I wasn't dreaming," he muttered, then glared up at the nurse. "What day is it?"

"February 13th," the Nurse replied.

"That can't be. I arrived in Scotland on January 30th, a couple of days before Imbolc." Confused and no longer certain of anything, Alex scratched his chin. "You said I had surgery. For what?" He couldn't argue the fact that he felt like he had an elephant sitting on his chest and the simplest movement caused him gut-wrenching pain, but he also recalled walking away from the crash virtually unscathed. They'd be hard pressed to convince him otherwise.

"You're lucky to be alive, Mr. Innes," the nurse said. "You sustained a hairline fracture of your scull with minor, controlled, intracranial bleeding and a severe concussion."

"That explains the pounding in my head, but not why my chest and the rest of my body feels like they're in a vice," Alex said. "The last thing I remember was being in the cave surrounding the well at Burghead. I was trying to rescue someone and toppled into the water. I hit my head on a rock, I'm guessing, blacked out, and woke up here."

The nurse frowned. "That is quite the tale. But you were brought here immediately following the crash and have not left that bed, other than to go down for a CT scan and a series of x-rays."

"It isn't a tale. It happened." Why wouldn't they believe him?

"In addition to the head trauma, you also suffered a ruptured spleen and a blunt chest injury, in which several of your ribs were fractured," the nurse continued to explain. "Your left lung was punctured by a rib fragment, causing a traumatic pneumothorax. A nick in the pericardial sack also resulted in cardiac tamponade. A buildup of fluid pressing on the heart," she added.

"The surgeon performed an emergency thoracotomy so he could remove the fragments of broken bones, repair the damage, set the ribs, and insert a catheter to drain the area around the lungs and heart. When finished in the chest cavity, he moved on to the abdomen and extricated your spleen."

Mrs. Innes rested her hand on Alex's forearm. "They had you in a drug induced coma until last night. They didn't want you thrashing about and reinjuring yourself. So you see dear, you were too ill to go anywhere."

"So you're telling me that I've been here for two weeks?" Alex blinked several times, finding it hard to believe he'd suffered so many injuries and lived. Was his time in the twelfth century a dream as his mother suggested? "Did anyone else survive the crash?"

The nurse hung her head. "Aye. The stewardess and one other passenger were found alive in the wreckage. The bairn, a seven year old lass, was airlifted to Glasgow, and we've had no further word on her condition."

The majority of passengers were adults, but Alex did remember seeing a little girl on the plane. She'd sat with a woman he'd assumed was her mother, three or four rows behind him. She had long golden ringlets and carried a rag doll he'd heard her refer to as Suzie when proudly showing her off to one of the flight attendants. He wondered if she was the child who survived. But so many others were not as lucky. The elderly couple who'd been sitting next to him came to mind. "And what about the flight attendant they rescued?"

The nurse shook her head. "I'm afraid that she succumbed to her injuries on the way to hospital."

He closed his eyes and muttered a prayer.

"It was a horrible tragedy. One that fortunately doesna happen often." The nurse checked the drainage bag attached to his chest tube before taking his blood pressure, then smiling. "Things appear stable and your chest is draining nicely. I'd suggest you get some rest and I'll inform Dr. Murray that you're awake. If you feel any sudden change in the level of pain or canna catch your breath, call immediately. I'll be at the nursing station if you need me."

Alex glanced at his mother. "You look exhausted. Why don't you go to the hotel and try and get some sleep. I'm obviously in good hands and it won't do either of us any good if you make yourself sick." While he was genuinely concerned about his mother's health, he needed some time to process everything he'd just learned. For the life of him he couldn't figure out why he was one of only two spared in the crash, and why the images of his time in the twelfth century were so vivid in his mind.

"Ciara." The word slipped out as if in prayer. Had she managed to keep the Talisman of Light and defeat the hag, or had Cailleach worked some other sorcery and won?

"What did you say, dear?" his mother asked. "It sounded like you said someone's name."

"It was nothing," he lied. He wished his mother could have met Ciara. She'd have adored her. Of that he was certain. But the meeting would never happen, because if what they told him about the crash was true, the love of his life didn't exist. Not in this century. Yet her memory left a gaping hole in his heart. One that no surgeon could repair.

"You really should go and get some rest, Mother. The drugs the nurse put in my IV are starting to work and I'm feeling punk. Once they take full effect, I'll likely sleep for hours and there is no point in you sitting here by yourself."

His mother smiled. "I doubt I'll be alone for long. A lovely young woman has been keeping me company. She was with you when the ambulance brought you in to the hospital."

He battled the drug-induced fog clouding him mind and causing his words to slur. "What woman? No one was meeting me at the airport and I was travelling alone."

"From what I was told, she wasn't on the plane, dear. She was one of those assisting with the rescue at the crash site," his mother replied. "When I arrived, you were still in surgery, and this very attractive young woman was waiting at your bedside for you to return to your room. A Scottish lass with a very sweet disposition and lovely green eyes. The nurse said she was in the ambulance with you and insisted on staying."

"Did she tell you her name?" Dare he hope?

"Why of course she did. Two women do not spend hours upon end together and not exchange names. She said her name was—"

"I'm so glad you're awake, Mr. Innes." A woman in a hooded cloak stood in the doorway. "You gave us all quite a fright."

Alex squinted, trying to focus on the woman, but the drugs were too powerful and he could no longer fight the inevitable.

Chapter Twelve

Alex awakened with a start. "God, I'm thirsty," He groaned, then covered his eyes with his forearm, shielding them from the blinding light above his bed.

"They don't want you to have anything to eat or drink yet, but the nurse left some ice in case you woke up and were thirsty," his mother said.

He stared up at his mother, grateful when she popped a couple of the chips into his mouth. "That is so good," Alex mumbled and sucked on the frozen morsels until they were gone. "What time is it? What day?"

"Why it's eight in the morning on the fourteenth. Valentine's Day to be exact," his mother said, grinning. "You slept through the entire night. Twelve hours." She glanced at her watch.

Alex scrubbed his fist across his eyes. He felt a little more human today, but still had a great deal of pain to contend with. His concern again shifted to his mother. "I hope you didn't sit there all night."

"I stayed until midnight, after which I went to a room they have set aside for the family of critical patients," she said. "But I didn't leave you alone. The young lady I was telling you about arrived just as you fell asleep. She stayed with you through the night."

Alex quickly scanned the room, but saw no one. "Did she leave?"

"When I returned to your room this morning she said she was going to freshen up and had a couple of things to tend to. I'm certain she won't be gone long. She never is."

"You didn't tell me her name." Alex grabbed his mother's hand and peered up at her. "Please, I need to know."

"Ciara Dunmore." A woman appeared at the door, carrying two large Styrofoam cups.

When the woman smiled, Alex's heart did a quick flip. "Ciara," he gasped. "Is it really you?"

"So you do know the lass," his mother said, grinning. She motioned with a flick of her hand. "Come in and sit a spell, Ciara. I was just telling Alex all about how you have not ventured far from his side since he was brought to hospital."

Ciara approached Alex's mother. "I was passing the coffee shop and thought you might like a cup. If you're hungry, I also have a bag of current scones in my purse."

"How thoughtful of you, dear." Mrs. Innes patted the chair beside her, then turned her attention back to Alex. "Isn't she lovely? Can you believe there was once a time when the Clan Innes and Clan Dunmore were enemies? Fortunately for you, that is no longer the case."

"Very fortunate," Alex mumbled, his eyes never leaving Ciara's face as she placed the cups on a table beside his mother before removing her coat. He studied her from top to bottom, half expecting her to be dressed in twelfth century attire. Instead, she wore a pair of loose-fitting grey tweed slacks, ankle-high suede boots, and a red turtleneck sweater that hugged her perfect breasts.

He swallowed hard as thoughts of how close they'd come to making love flooded his mind. Alex gave his head a shake. While the woman indeed looked like the Ciara he'd spent the last couple of days getting to know, there was something different about this woman. She carried herself with confidence. She dressed and spoke in a manor more in tune with the twenty-first century, not the twelfth. Since she didn't immediately run to his side or show any indication of affection, he decided to wait and compare the similarities and differences between the Ciara in his room and the one from the past before saying any more.

But when she approached the bed and touched his hand, a familiar, tingling sensation ran up his arm, warming his heart. He knew instantly this was his Ciara.

"Is something wrong?" his mother asked.

Alex wanted to grab Ciara by hand, draw her closer, and kiss her, but he refrained from doing so. "Enemies you say?"

"Aye, and all because of ancient superstition and this." She reached into the neck of her sweater and tugged on a chain, revealing an amulet made of rubies—identical to the Talisman of Light Alex had carried back to Scotland and given to Ciara as she was about to face Cailleach for the last time.

"That's a lovely antique." Barely able to contain his excitement at seeing the gem, Alex nipped at his bottom lip.

"It dates back to at least the twelfth century." Ciara fondled it lovingly. "This has been in my family for hundreds of years. Passed down from mother to daughter." Her brow creased as she stared at the gem. "It was missing for a while, but miraculously turned up recently. Some say it has magical powers and is linked to the Imbolc Festival that recently took place at the end of February in hopes of an early spring. They claim it was used to defeat the winter hag. But that is just legend, of course."

"You should wear it always," Alex said."

"I never plan to take it off again. Not unless I have a daughter to pass it on to someday." She tucked it back into the neck of her sweater.

His heart sank. "You're married?"

"Nay. I was too busy getting my practice off the ground to think about marriage and a family of my own," she replied. "But if the right man came along, I might consider it."

"Our patient needs to rest." A different nurse from the one yesterday appeared at the door. "He's had enough stimulation for one morning, and the medication I added to his IV half an hour ago should have taken affect by now."

Alex yawned, struggling to stay awake. He feared he was losing the battle, but he had to talk to Ciara, *alone*.

"Perhaps we'll have to increase the dosage," the nurse said. "We are very careful with pain medication in patients with compromised respiratory function. They can slow the heart rate and interfere with the ability to breathe, neither of which Mr. Innes needs." She glanced at her watch. "However, he does need to rest."

The nurse studied the chart hanging at the foot of Alex's bed, then checked the monitors. "A patient can become resistant to the meds over time. I'll page Dr. Murray and see if he wants to up the dosage. In the meantime, if you ladies are in need of a break, the solarium in the hospital's enclosed courtyard is lovely at this time of day. And if you get hungry, the cafeteria's lunch special is Shepherd's Pie." She turned and left the room.

"It sounds wonderful and I'm sure the nurse is right. You could use a break, Mrs. Innes, and Alex needs his sleep." Ciara cupped his mother's elbow. "Shall we get a bit of sun?"

"Fine, but I'm not leaving the hospital. Not until my son is out of ICU and has been given a clean bill of health from Dr. Murray." After grabbing her purse and her cup of coffee, Mrs. Innes leaned over the bed and kissed Alex on the cheek. "I won't be gone long. Do as the nurse tell you and I will see if I can talk them into giving you some Jell-O for dinner."

Alex chuckled as he watched his mother head toward the door, with Ciara at her heel. Deloris Innes was never going to change. No matter how old he got, she'd always see him as her little boy. He had to admit, he was grateful for her love and devotion. To see the two women he cared about more than life itself bonding made his heart soar. But he had to find out if Ciara remembered him, aside from the crash. Why else would she stay by his side? Did she feel the same connection and bond to the past that he felt? He had to know.

"Can I see you for a moment in private, Ciara?"

She glanced over her shoulder, a puzzled expression crossing her face. "Certainly. I'll join you in a minute, Mrs. Innes."

"I've told you to call me Deloris. And take all the time you'd like, dear." She smiled at Alex and winked. "I'll be waiting at the nursing station," she said as she left the room.

"What did you want?" Ciara returned to his bedside.

"When did we meet, and why did you stay with my mother?" Almost afraid to hear the answer, Alex chewed on the inside of his cheek.

"I was at the crash site right after the plane went down, helping to evacuate the passengers and tending to the injured."

"So you're a doctor or EMT?"

"I'm a Nurse Practitioner and Registered Midwife with an office in Burghead," she replied. "I was in Inverness at a medical conference when I heard about the crash on the radio. I wasna far, so I figured with my medical training I might be of some help."

"You're a healer?" The similarities between this Ciara and the one from the past mounted. In fact they were downright conclusive as far as Alex was concerned.

She chuckled. "Some of the older members of my clan call me that, but the university I attended frowns on such antiquated titles."

Her smile lit up the room and he wanted to leap from the bed, haul her into his arms, and kiss her senseless, unleashing the passion he'd harnessed since they met. But that would not only be impossible in his condition, but foolish. He didn't want to frighten her.

"You just happened to be there when they extracted me from the wreckage?" Alex inquired.

"Aye. They found you in a section near the wing. The only portions of the plane still intact. You were fortunate to be seated where you were." she said. "According to the men who pulled you out, you were suspended upside-down, trapped in your seatbelt."

"Hard to believe they found me alive," Alex sighed. "So when did we actually meet for the first time? Why did you stay with me? I would imagine you have a busy practice and are needed there."

"We didn't actually meet formally. You were unconscious at the time and in very bad shape." She touched the back of his hand, but quickly withdrew her fingers as if she'd burnt them. "As for staying, I felt compelled to see this through. I had some vacation time coming and have a very competent replacement covering for me in my absence. Why is when we met so important?"

She felt the connection between them. Alex was certain of it. But he still was not quite ready to disclose his secret, fearing that if he was wrong, she'd think him mad. "I just wondered why a stranger would stay with someone they didn't know."

She shifted her weight from one foot to the other, as if being so close to him made her nervous. "There was so much going on following the crash, and all of the emergency personnel were needed to search for survivors. I offered to accompany you in the ambulance to the hospital."

"I'm grateful. But that still doesn't explain why you stayed after you got me here safely?" He clasped her hand.

"I...dinna know," she stammered and tried to tug free, but he tightened his grip.

"Do you believe in fate and destiny, Ciara?"

"I come from a village steeped in archaic beliefs and superstition. A place that still burns the Clavie and parades it through town to celebrate the New Year, then collects the charred pieces to ward off evil. Unlike the rest of Scotland, they celebrate on the eleventh of January, in accordance with the Julian calendar and not on the first day of the month. I live amongst people who believe in magic, spells, and pagan rituals." She smiled. "Some of that is bound to rub off."

"Then you believe it is possible for a person's fate to be pre-determined?" He hoped she'd agree. He wanted to tell her the truth. "Do you believe two people could know each other in another place and time, another century even, yet somehow find each other again in the present?"

"I'm a woman of science. I believe in medical facts and—"

"You didn't answer my question. Do you believe in love that can transcend the barriers of time?"

"Why are you asking me these questions?" Her eyes downcast, she wrenched free of his grasp and wrapped her arms around her middle. "Do you believe it's possible?"

"If you'd asked me before I got on that plane, I'd have said no, without a doubt in my mind. But now, I'm not so certain."

"What made you change your mind?" She edged closer.

The nurse returned, carrying a syringe. "I spoke to Dr. Murray. Given your miraculous improvement and stable vitals, he has ordered me to double the dose of sedatives." She moved to the IV pole, clamped off the smaller of the two bags, and laid it on the instrument table beside the monitors. "I'll add this and you'll be asleep in no time."

"Can't it wait just a few more minutes?" Alex asked. "Ciara and I were in the middle of a very important conversation and we need to finish. Please."

"Dr. Murray is afraid of a relapse if you overdo it." The nurse glanced from Alex to Ciara and back. "I suppose a few minutes willna matter. I remember what it was like to be young and in love. But only if you promise to go to sleep as soon as I add the medication to the IV."

"You are still a young, attractive woman," Alex said, grinning. He figured a little flattery might help his cause.

The nurse blushed and dismissed his comment with the

wave of her hand. "I turned fifty last month and I'll na be bamboozled by sweet talking, Mr. Innes. You have five minutes and I'll be back." She rehung the medicine bag and retrieved the syringe before leaving. "Five minutes!"

"She runs a tight ship," Alex chuckled.

"The nurse is doing her job and you are not making it easy on her," Ciara countered. "All the more reason for me to go. Besides, your mother is waiting for me." She turned to leave.

"Don't go, Ciara. We haven't finished our conversation."

"It can wait." She headed for the door again.

"No, it can't. I need to finish this now, or I can never rest," he said, hoping she would feel sorry for him, and if nothing else, remain long enough for him to ask a favor.

Ciara threw her hands in the air and ambled back to the bed. "This discussion is going around in circles and accomplishing nothing. We have established how we met, and that you need your rest. I think that is enough for now."

"Grant me one request and I'll let you leave. I promise if you do, I'll not bring this up again." In a last ditch effort, he offered her a pleading glance. "Cross my heart. I will not bring it up again unless you wish me to."

She folded her arms over her chest and glared down at him. "Fine. What is your one request?"

"Kiss me."

"I beg your pardon?"

He wasn't sure if she looked shocked or appalled. But he repeated it anyway. "I want you to kiss me."

Chapter Thirteen

Shocked by his request, Ciara stared back at Alex. "Why on earth would you ask me to kiss you? We only just met." She backed away from the bed. "I'm na in the habit of kissing strangers."

He held his hand out to her. "Trust me, Ciara, we are not strangers."

"I dinna know you, Alex"

"I think you do. In fact, I know you do. Better than you are willing to admit. We fell in love in the past and could again if given a chance," Alex said. "Kiss me and perhaps we will both have an answer. It might jog your memory."

"This is insane. Why are you so sure we knew each other in a past life?" she asked. "What if I did know you, but dinna want to remember?" She couldn't believe she was asking such ludicrous questions. *Or were they?*

"I don't blame you for thinking I'm nuts," Alex began. "And if you ran out of here right now and never looked back, you'd be well within your rights. I can't explain how I know what I do to be the truth, but I feel it here—" Alex lightly thumped his fist against his chest. "The moment I laid eyes upon you at the crash site, I felt that there was a connection between us. You must believe me, Ciara. We did know each other in the past, and are meant to be together."

"I've never heard of such a foolish thing in all my life." Ciara glanced away. Despite what logic dictated, she too had experienced a strange, yet familiar bond with Alex. As if the energy she felt flowing between them when she touched his hand somehow joined them together. Nor could she explain why she was compelled to stay with a total stranger once he was admitted to hospital. But with those warm feelings of affection and familiarity came a sense of foreboding she couldn't shake either.

Though reluctant to admit it, Ciara did believe in destiny. She was raised on Celtic superstition and the ancient legends of the past. She believed in honoring time-honored traditions, and contrary to what many claimed to be fraudulent or a myth, she was convinced, witches, fairies, demons, and things like the gift of second sight did exist.

If truth be known, she often had dreams about dwelling in the past. Some were so vivid, she awakened in a panic, and was certain her experiences were real. In spite of being raised in the twenty-first century, she often felt awkward and alone, prompting her to wonder if she hadn't been displaced and belonged in an era from the past. But she'd kept this bottled up inside, never sharing it with anyone.

How could Alex know about it?

Ciara wanted to believe that true love could stand the test of time and could even be reborn. However, desire could not overpower common sense, and she refused to fall victim to the rantings of a man who had clearly lost his mind.

"I suggest you forget this notion and get some rest as the nurse suggested," Ciara said. "What you ask will prove nothing."

"You will never know unless you kiss me. What have you got to lose?"

"My sanity." She hesitated at first, but soon found herself moving forward. She leaned over the bed. "I dinna know what good this will do, and am sure I'll live to regret it. But if it means you will drop this interrogation, so be it."

Alex cupped her cheek with his hand, her hair tumbling forward and brushing the back of it. He gently tucked the errant locks behind her ear and urged her closer, until their mouths were but a breath away.

"You're so lovely, you render me speechless." Alex gazed into her eyes as he swept the pad of his thumb across her lips. "If after we kiss, you don't feel something so potent you can't catch your breath, I'll not ask again."

"It's a deal." Ciara muttered and closed her eyes.

He tickled her pursed lips with his tongue, willing them to open. She inhaled deeply, his woodsy male scent more intoxicating than the mulled wine she loved so much. Aware that this was wrong, Ciara knew she should put an end to it immediately, yet she couldn't bring herself to do so.

As he began to nibble on her bottom lip, he wove his fingers through her hair, holding her head in place. Alex was right, there was something tangible between them and while his kiss was chaste at first, an array of wondrous sensations she'd never experienced before erupted from her core, flooding her mind, body and soul. Her legs suddenly felt like jelly so she planted her hands on the bed for support. Her pulse quickened, her heart thumping so loudly, she was certain he could hear it beating in unison with his own.

She'd dated in the past and had even met a couple of men she thought she might grow to love. But no one had ever kissed her like this, nor did she want it to end. She released a soft sigh and granted him entry. He plundered her mouth, kissing her with the desperation of a man whose very life depended on it. Their tongues tangled in an intimate dance, then without warning he broke the connection between them.

"Well?" he asked on a strangled breath. "Did you feel it?"

"I-I dinna know what to say, what to think." She straightened her shoulders, her fingers lightly tracing where his lips had been, a blend of excitement, unbridled passion, and fear washing over her.

He smiled. "You don't have to say anything. Your eyes and the way you responded speak for you."

Ciara shook her head. "You're wrong, Alex. I—"

"Am I? Can you look at me and deny what transpired between us?" He grasped her hand and brought it to his lips, kissing the back of it. "Close your eyes, Ciara. It's okay to remember the past, to accept that fate has reunited us. Had I not experienced it for myself, I wouldn't have believed it either. But the heart doesn't lie."

"This is all so much to take in at once." Ciara wrung her hands and began to pace. "This is crazy. People who lived in the past do not fall in love and reunite in the future. It just doesna happen."

"But it did happen, sweeting." Alex said. "It is a lot to fathom and you can take all the time you need. When you're ready, we'll talk about what was and what can be."

"If what you claim is true...And I'm not saying it is," Ciara quickly added. "How can you be so sure we were meant to be together?"

"I know because the amulet is where it belongs and we are both alive and have a chance to continue where we left off."

Ciara clutched the pendant. "What do you know about the amulet?

"It was crafted by the druids and meant to appease Cailleach, the winter hag on Imbolc, to bribe her into sparing the life of the Dunmore maiden and release the land from winter's grip," Alex said. "But it was hidden and then stolen. If it had not been returned at least one maiden and perhaps many more would have been sacrificed, changing our history entirely."

"How do you know this?" Ciara asked.

"Not only am I an archeologist, I experienced it firsthand," Alex said. "But the talisman is back where it belongs and regardless of what happens from here on in, it will always be safe. Just like our secret. A foundation we can build upon or a memory we can cherish." Alex clasped her hand again. "But I do have one more request. There was something I asked you right after the plane crashed, and you never gave me an answer."

She brought a hand to her throat. "What might that be?"

Alex's grin broadened. "Once I'm out of the hospital and on the mend, will you have dinner with me? I'd like to take you to your favorite restaurant as my way of saying thank you for all you've done for me and for my mother. I'd also like a chance to get to know you again. I fell in love with the Ciara from the past, but something tells me I am going to adore the Ciara of the present. Will you give us a chance, see where this might lead?"

Ciara pondered his request for a moment and smiled. "I'd like that very much. I do think you might make a believer out of me yet, Alex Innes." She leaned down and kissed him again.

"I hate to interrupt, but all good things must come to an end," the nurse said as she entered the room.

"You're wrong," Alex said. "This is only the beginning."

character. It's a shame she never married or had any children."

"No. I didn't know her well." Katherine sucked in a cleansing breath to settle her nerves before continuing. "When I was seven-years old, Aunt Agnes paid a visit to my family's New England home. Unfortunately, it was the only time we met. But my maternal grandmother, Margaret, who was my aunt's only sister, often said I was the spitting-image of Agnes when she was a child. Even though I inherited my father's dark hair."

"You must have been a very comely bairn. I'm told your aunt was quite breathtaking."

The heat of embarrassment rose in Katherine's cheeks. She wasn't fishing for compliments. "Aunt Agnes was much lovelier than I could ever hope to be." She closed her eyes, picturing her great-aunt's Titian hair piled high on her head, her wide green eyes, and sweet, yet mischievous smile. To say they looked alike was an exaggeration as far as Katherine was concerned.

She'd never considered herself to be a beautiful woman by most modern standards. While Katherine prided herself in being physically fit, her slender—almost boyish figure—lack of buxom feminine curves, her aversion for too much makeup, passable facial features, and the dusting of freckles across her nose was far from model material. She saw herself as average looking, more like the girl-next-door than a raving beauty. A woman most men smiled at, asked out for a drink, but never longed to possess. Eye-candy she wasn't.

She'd often wondered why Ethan asked her to marry him. Especially when he could have any beautiful Manhattan debutant of his choosing. Was it her intelligence, ingenuity, and keen knack for business that intrigued him? Or was it her reluctance to fall for his charm when they first met? He often fixated on things that were out of his reach. And with her aversion to relationships, she did present a challenge.

True, she had her share of date offers, but finishing her education and the drive to succeed in her chosen profession overshadowed her desire for fun and frivolity—the very things on which Agnes reportedly thrived. Structure, hard work, and responsibility were traits her father instilled in her from the time she was very young. But Katherine secretly wished she had just a touch of adventure in her life.

She smiled, remembering the wonderful tales Agnes told about the faeries, kelpies, selkies, and other fae creatures who occupied the Highland forests and waterways. But they were just that, stories meant to entertain children and those foolish enough to believe in, superstition, romance, and happily-ever-after endings.

"So your mam was a Grant, I take it?" The receptionist licked the seal of a rose-colored envelope and pressed it closed before adding it to a pile of outgoing mail in front of her.

Her question interrupted, Katherine's musing. She had never been one for small talk with strangers, but she decided it was better than sitting there in silence or thinking about Ethan. "My maternal grandmother was Agnes's younger sister. She was a Grant until she moved to the United States and married my grandfather, Harold Lindsay. They had one daughter, Moira, and she was my mother."

"I see," the receptionist stroked her chin. "And your da? Is he an American?"

"He was born in Hartford Connecticut, but he had Scottish roots too. His name was Hunter MacDonald. He was an architect in Boston, and—" Katherine bowed her head.

"Was, dear?" The receptionist asked.

"My parents both died in an automobile accident when I was sixteen. They were hit by a drunk driver. After that, I went to live with my grandmother, but she has also passed on." Katherine wiped a tear from her cheek with the back of her hand, then coughed. Talking about her family always caused her throat to thicken with emotion.

The receptionist rose, rounded her desk, and handed Katherine a tissue. "I'm sorry for your loss. According to Ms. Grant's file, you were listed as the only beneficiary of her will. I'm assuming from what you've said, you were also an only bairn, and there are no other living relatives on your mother's side of the family."

Katherine almost choked on the words. "That's correct. I had no brothers or sisters."

"Are you married, lass?"

Katherine balled the tissue in her fist, her gaze fixed on the floor. She swallowed hard. "And there is no one of significance in my life."

"I'm surprised a lovely lass like you hasna married," the receptionist said.

When her parents died, followed by her grandmother two years later, Katherine was left alone. They'd been her whole life and she missed them terribly, the deep ache of loss devouring her heart and leaving her chest an empty void.

Determined to guard herself from further pain, she concentrated on her studies, vowing never to fall in love. She had plenty of friends and acquaintances, but eventually realized it wasn't enough. Unfortunately, the one time she broke her hard and fast rule of never getting into a relationship proved to be a disaster.

"Is this your first trip to Scotland?" the receptionist asked.

"Yes. I always planned to visit, but never got the chance." And, she wouldn't be here now if she wasn't trying to escape from her abusive fiancé.

After graduating from university with honors and a Master's Degree in business administration and marketing, Katherine was thrilled to snag a job with the prestigious Cochran Advertising Agency—leaving her little time for a social life and even less time to think about the fact that she was very much alone. But meeting Ethan changed all that.

Refusing to dwell on her past mistakes or to wallow in self-pity, Katherine abruptly rose to her feet and approached the receptionist. "I don't mean to be rude, but I've waited long enough and my time is valuable. Have Mr. MacBain or Mr. Murray call me when they would like to reschedule my appointment." She grabbed a notepad and pen from atop the desk and jotted down her cell number. "They can reach me at—"

The phone rang and the receptionist answered it. "Aye Mr. Murray." She replaced the receiver on the cradle and smiled at Katherine. "If you can abide a wee longer, they'll be ready for you soon."

"Fine." Katherine stomped back to her chair and sat. But a few minutes to MacBain and Murray seemed like yet another lifetime. Her eyelids growing heavy, she rested her forehead upon her hand. "Maybe if I shut my eyes for just a minute, I'll feel better," she mumbled.

~ * ~

A warm breeze caressed her cheek and Katherine tipped her face toward the sun, hoping to catch the warmth of its rays. Lifting the hem of her ivory colored gown she dipped her bare toes into the loch, then withdrew them quickly, the water still frigid from winter's grip.

With arms outstretched, she spun full circle, taking in the panoramic beauty of the burn, the glen, and mountains around her. Fragrant heather dotted the brae and meadow, along with bluebells and other assorted wildflowers. Highland cows and sheep grazed on sweet tender shoots of grass and a pair of hawks circled in unison overhead, in what she guessed was a mating ritual as old as time.

Spring had always been Katherine's favorite time of year and this one had proved to be more glorious than others she recalled.

B.J. Scott

"I nary tire of looking at you, lass. You always manage to take my breath away." A warrior wearing a chainmail tunic, padded gambeson, trews, and leather gauntlets rode into the clearing on a black destrier. He quickly dismounted and strode toward her with purpose. "Have you been here long, ma gaol?"

Katherine smiled up at him. "Long enough. I am na a lass who likes to be kept waiting. You're lucky I dinna leave before you arrived," she answered playfully.

"Is that so? Then, you'd have missed out on this." He slid his arm around her waist, drew her against his chest, and nipped at her lower lip. "And this." He buried his head in the curve of her neck, suckled lightly, then feathered kisses upward until he reached her mouth.

Enveloped in warmth and bombarded by desire that ravaged her body like a wildfire out of control, she leaned into his embrace, her stomach doing a quick flip and moist heat pooling between her thighs. Her knees suddenly weak, she fisted his tunic for support. "You know it is na easy to get away from home and na have my da or meddlesome brother follow me," she mumbled against his lips, then kissed his cheek.

"When we're married, you'll only answer to one man." He lowered his head and nibbled at her bottom lip again. "Me." A possessive growl rumbled in his chest as he tightened his hold and kissed her soundly. He slid the tip of his tongue across her mouth, willing her to open to his sweet invasion. When she gasped with pleasure, he deepened the kiss, plundering without mercy.

Breathless, she planted her hands on his chest and shoved until their kiss was broken. "If we marry." She lifted gaze until it met with his, then slowly took in the contours of his finely chiseled features. He was the handsomest man she'd ever seen and what he could do to her insides with just his presence had to be a sin. But he was not her father's choice for a husband.

His brows dipped. "Dinna toy with me, lass. You know we're meant to be together and it's only a matter of time afore we wed," he replied. "In fact, I plan to speak with your da this evening at the feast. I'm going to ask for your hand and his permission to marry you before the garrison heads out to challenge the English bastards who threaten to take Stirling Castle."

"When do you leave?" She clung to his shirt.

"Two days hence."

She clutched a hand to a knot of emotion choking her throat. "Why even if my father did agree to our union, there isna enough time to have the banns read."

"We can dispense with the reading if the priest so chooses. And if I have my way, by this time on the morrow, we'll be husband and wife." His brows shot up and mischievous grin tugged at his lips. "And after a night of wedded bliss, you'll be glad to see me go, thankful for the rest."

"What if the priest refuses or my da says nay?"

A stern expression darkened his features, his gaze intense. "Leave your da to me. I'll have no talk about what if. Na when we have this time alone together now," he said, his voice hard edged. Wasting no time, he scooped her into his arms and carried her to patch of soft grass beneath an old oak tree and gently lay her upon it. "You're mine and let no man say otherwise."

When he sprawled out beside her and pulled her into his embrace, Katherine offered no resistance. Instead, she lightly traced his lips with her fingertips and sighed. "If truth be known, I want to marry you more than my next breath, and will do whatever it takes for us to be together."

And why wouldn't she welcome their union? He was the oldest son of a laird and stood to be a chieftain someday. Not that she cared about title or wealth. It was the man inside that she adored, not what he had to offer in the way of land or riches. But he was fine to look at. He was tall, well-muscled, brave and honorable, yet treated her with the utmost gentleness and reverence. He looked upon her as his equal, not his property—rare for a man in his day. The fact he was a braw feast for her eyes to behold and could turn her inside out with merely a glance, didn't hurt either. Theirs was a marriage made in heaven.

So why wasn't she thrilled about the prospects of becoming his wife?

She frowned, a feeling of dread twisting her gut. Something from deep in the recesses of her soul told her their marriage would never take place, not without much hardship and heartache.

He stroked her cheek with the pad of his thumb. "What troubles you, sweeting?"

Tears welled in her eyes and she blinked them away. "I dinna wish for you to go with the warriors to Stirling. I fear something terrible will befall you there, and we might na see each other again."

"What would you have me do? I'm a son of Scotland. It's my duty to defend her soil. I promise to return to you."

He rolled her beneath him, lowered his head, and captured her lips.

~ * ~

"Mr. MacBain and Mr. Murray are ready to see you now?" The secretary touched her shoulder. "It appears you nodded off."

Katherine yawned and stretched. Part of her wanted to wake up, yet part of her wanted to stay asleep forever. This wasn't the first time she'd had this dream. And something told her she belonged with her dashing knight, in another place and time. The vastness of her emotions and love for this figment of her imagination was how a relationship between a man and woman should be. But he was from the 14th Century and she was from the twenty-first. An impossible scenario to say the least. Hell, she didn't even know his name.

The secretary pointed to the door. "They're waiting for you, my dear."

"Now, they're in a freaking hurry," Katherine grumbled and stood. But as she approached the door, she heard the raised voices of the two men. They appeared to be engaged in a heated argument.

"Nay, Duncan, the requirements are verra clear. For the lass to inherit the croft, she must comply with the terms outlined in her aunt's will," one man said.

"I'm aware of what the document dictates, Malcolm. However, the lass isna from Scotland and might na be willing to abide by her aunt's requests. In which case, all will be lost," the other man countered.

"Aye, what you're saying is true, Duncan, but we are bound by the terms stipulated and the lass must prove herself worthy. If she refused, we canna—"

Katherine knocked on the door and pushed it open before either of the men had a chance to respond. "I don't mean to interrupt, but the secretary told me you were ready to see me. I'm Katherine MacDonald."

Other Titles from Duncurra

Lily Baldwin

The Highland Outlaw Series

Jack: A Scottish Outlaw (Book 1)
Quinn: A Scottish Outlaw (Book 2)
Rory: A Scottish Outlaw (Book 3)
Alex: A Scottish Outlaw (Book 4) – coming soon

The Isle of Mull Series

To Bewitch a Highlander (Book 1)
Highland Thunder (Book 2)
To Love a Warrior (Book 3)

Flights of Love Series

A Jewel in the Vaults (Flights of Love Series, Book 1)

Beautiful Darkness Series

Highland Shadows (Beautiful Darkness Series, Book 1)

Stephanie Joyce Cole

Compass North

New York Times Bestselling Author
Kathryn Lynn Davis

Highland Awakening
Sing to Me of Dreams
Weave for Me a Dream – Coming in March 2017

Award Winning, Bestselling Author
Ceci Giltenan

The Pocket Watch Chronicles

The Pocket Watch

The Midwife

Once Found

The Christmas Present

The Choice – Coming Soon

The Fated Hearts Series

Highland Revenge

Highland Echoes

Highland Angels

The Duncurra Series

Highland Solution

Highland Courage

Highland Intrigue

Ford Murphy

Taking the Town

MJ Platt

Somewhere Montana

www.ingramcontent.com/pod-product-compliance
Lightning Source LLC
Chambersburg PA
CBHW020406130626
46549CB00006B/2461